THE LEGACY SERIES

SERIES TITLES

I Felt My Life With Both My Hands
Jessica Treadway

Hands
Pardeep Toor

Lafferty, Looking for Love
Dennis McFadden

This Is How We Speak
Rebecca Reynolds

All That It Seems
Jim Landwehr

All Gone Now
Michael Tasker

Your Place in This World
Jake La Botz

Apple & Palm
Patricia Henley

Bodies in Bags
Jamey Gallagher

A Green Glow on the Horizon
Dawn Burns

How We Do Things Here
Matt Cashion

Neon Steel
Jennifer Maritza McCauley

Release of Information
Kali White VanBaale

The Divide
Evan Morgan Williams

Yes, No, I Don't Know
Kathryn Gahl

The Price of Their Toys
John Loonam

The Caged Man
Calvin Mills

A Day Doesn't Go By When I Don't Have Regrets
J. Malcolm Garcia

These Are My People
Steve Fox

We Should Be Somewhere by Now
Stephen Tuttle

Burner and Other Stories
Katrina Denza

The Plan of Chicago
Barry Pearce

Trust Issues
K.P. Davis

Adult Children
Laurence Klavan

Guardians & Saints
Diane Josefowicz

Western Terminus: Stories and A Novella
Michael Keefe

Like Human
Janet Goldberg

The Hopefuls
Elizabeth Oness

Never Stop Exiting
Michael Hopkins

Broken Heart Syndrome
Anne Colwell

The Mexican Messiah: A Novella & Stories
Jay Kauffmann

Close to a Flame
Colleen Alles

American Animism
Jamey Gallagher

Keeping What's Best Left Kept Secret
David Ricchiute

Soaked
Toby LeBlanc

The Path of Totality
Marie Zhuikov

Shocker in Gloomtown
Dan Libman

The Continental Divide
Bob Johnson

The Three Devils and Other Stories
William Luvaas

The Correct Response
Manfred Gabriel

Welcome Back to the World: A Novella & Stories
Rob Davidson

Greyhound Cowboy and Other Stories
Ken Post

Close Call
Kim Suhr

The Waterman
Gary Schanbacher

Signs of the Imminent Apocalypse and Other Stories
Heidi Bell

What We Might Become
Sara Reish Desmond

The Silver State Stories
Michael Darcher

An Instinct for Movement
Michael Mattes

The Machine We Trust
Tim Conrad

Gridlock
Brett Biebel

Salt Folk
Ryan Habermeyer

The Commission of Inquiry
Patrick Nevins

Maximum Speed
Kevin Clouther

Reach Her in This Light
Jane Curtis

The Spirit in My Shoes
John Michael Cummings

The Effects of Urban Renewal on Mid-Century America and Other Crime Stories
Jeff Esterholm

What Makes You Think You're Supposed to Feel Better
Jody Hobbs Hesler

Fugitive Daydreams
Leah McCormack

Hoist House: A Novella & Stories
Jenny Robertson

Finding the Bones: Stories & A Novella
Nikki Kallioy

Self-Defense
Corey Mertes

Where Are Your People From?
James B. De Monte

Sometimes Creek
Steve Fox

The Plagues
Joe Baumann

The Clayfields
Elise Gregory

Kind of Blue
Christopher Chambers

Evangelina Everyday
Dawn Burns

Township
Jamie Lyn Smith

Responsible Adults
Patricia Ann McNair

Great Escapes from Detroit
Joseph O'Malley

Nothing to Lose
Kim Suhr

The Appointed Hour
Susanne Davis

PRAISE FOR
Jessica Treadway

"Treadway's stories reveal a writer with an unsparing bent for the truth."

—*THE NEW YORK TIMES BOOK REVIEW*

"Treadway examines and exposes emotions that few would readily admit to."

—*PUBLISHERS WEEKLY*

"Treadway's prose is clear and searingly direct."

—*THE BOSTON GLOBE*

"Treadway is at her best when she depicts characters colliding with one another in the blind clutch of life."

—*THE RUMPUS*

"In *I Felt My Life With Both My Hands*, a moving, thoughtful and heartfelt collection, ordinary people and ordinary encounters yield extraordinary moments of insight and inspiration. What a lovely, loving book! Highly recommended."

—GISH JEN
author of *Bad Bad Girl*

"The women who narrate the remarkable stories in Jessica Treadway's *I Felt My Life With Both My Hands* find the same kinds of hopes and sorrows filling and emptying their hearts—overtaking or abandoning them with power so startling but so intimately familiar that we recognize on every page our own sense of how often we are strangers most of all to ourselves."

—PAUL HARDING
Pulitzer Prize Winner
author of *Tinkers*

"I can't remember a story collection that has stirred my heart so strongly and made me feel so deeply for its characters as *I Felt My Life With Both My Hands*. Beautifully written, complex, and oh so smart."

—EILEEN POLLACK
author of *In the Mouth*

"Treadway awakens us to the marvel of our ordinary lives."

—E.J. LEVY
author of *The Cape Doctor*

"Treadway is masterful."

—LILY KING
author of *Euphoria*

"I know of few authors who can write with the intelligence, sensitivity, and grace of Jessica Treadway. I know of none who can write with such courage."

—ELIZABETH BERG
author of *Earth's the Right Place for Love*

I FELT MY LIFE WITH BOTH MY HANDS *stories*

JESSICA TREADWAY

CORNERSTONE PRESS
UNIVERSITY OF WISCONSIN-STEVENS POINT

Cornerstone Press, Stevens Point, Wisconsin 54481
Copyright © 2026 Jessica Treadway
www.uwsp.edu/cornerstone

Printed in the United States of America.

Library of Congress Control Number: 2026930482
ISBN: 978-1-968148-37-9

All rights reserved.

Cover art: Edward Hopper, "Cape Cod Morning," 1950 © 2025 Heirs of Josephine N. Hopper / Licensed by Artists Rights Society (ARS), NY

This is a work of fiction. Names, characters, businesses, places, events, and incidents are either the products of the author's imagination or used in a fictitious manner. Any resemblance to actual persons, living or dead, or actual events is purely coincidental.

Cornerstone Press titles are produced in courses and internships offered by the Department of English at the University of Wisconsin–Stevens Point.

Director & Publisher	Executive Editors
Dr. Ross K. Tangedal	Jeff Snowbarger, Freesia McKee
Editorial Director	Senior Editors
Brett Hill	Paige Biever, Ellie Atkinson

Press Staff
Samantha Bjork, Sophie McPherson, Nathan Pearson, Hannah Rouer, Lilli Resop, Aja Wooley, Madison Schultz, Autumn Vine

In loving memory of Andre Dubus

(1936–1999)—

Friend, inspiration, and master of the form

ALSO BY JESSICA TREADWAY:

Infinite Dimensions
The Gretchen Question
How Will I Know You?
Lacy Eye
Please Come Back To Me
And Give You Peace
Absent Without Leave

STORIES

The Boy on the Skateboard 1

Ride Share 9

An Early Departure 24

First Day 34

Cliché 43

Tribute 60

Attached 71

An Interest in History 80

Take What You Want 88

Infusion 100

Undefeated 108

The Forest 120

The Daughter's Story 129

Cri de Coeur 169

Acknowledgments 185

Possibly it's something women do: spend time imagining what it's like to be each other. One can learn from that, he thinks.

—Hilary Mantel, *Wolf Hall*

The Boy on the Skateboard

"There he is again," my mother said, pointing out the window. "The boy on the skateboard. Hey, that would make a good title. Will you write that story? For me?"

She'd said things like this before, but in a kidding tone. This time, she sounded as if she meant it. I told her "Sure," even though there was nothing about the boy that interested or intrigued me enough that I would have thought to write about him without my mother's request. He didn't pique my imagination in any way. I didn't wonder anything about him as I often wondered about people I observed in the world and then used as templates for characters in my fiction.

Like the woman I saw at the gym every time I went, who routinely climbed the stair-stepper so rapidly and for so long that sweat dripped off her and pooled on the floor around the machine. Her eyes were closed and her face tilted toward the ceiling in what might have looked like rapture if you couldn't see how much exertion it took to keep up with the pace she'd programmed. *She's punishing herself*, I thought. One day I sat down and wrote a story about a woman who drinks a pint of vodka every night because it's the only way she can fall asleep, wakes up reeling, and heads to the gym to sweat out the poison she's poured in herself. To sweat out her sin.

The boy on the skateboard was almost not even a boy at all—he might have been sixteen. To be honest, I formed the quick impression that he was something of a punk, with long hair he didn't bother to sweep out of his eyes. If not exactly a punk, then an unremarkable teenager. Twice a day that weekend, he glided up the driveway of the house next door, went around to the back, uncoiled the long hose from its spool, and sent a long, wobbly spray over some kind of garden—flower or vegetable I couldn't tell.

My mother lay on the couch under an afghan my grandmother, her own mother, had knitted for me when I was a baby. It wasn't big enough to cover an adult, and I offered to find something else for her, but that was the one she wanted.

We spent a lot of time that weekend watching TV. A couple of times a day I convinced her to go out to the driveway with me, to walk to the end and back per the surgeon's instructions. I fixed high-calorie meals for both of us, because she needed to put some weight back on, and I made up a chart so she'd know when to take her medications after I had to leave.

It was nice, like the old days when I lived there with her. I know we both felt that way. I told her I wished I could stay longer, and it was true. She understood that I had to get back to my job. I was still only an adjunct, at two different schools, and I couldn't afford to miss any classes. In some ways it would have been easier if she'd acted more needy or begged me to stay. Then I could have resented her. As it was, I already felt regretful and guilty. But I tried to set that aside and make the most of the weekend we had together.

We watched so much TV because her energy was still low from the eight days she'd spent in the hospital. I tried to persuade her to choose movies or sitcom episodes we could order on demand, because the news was filled with unhappy stories, so much hatred in so many forms. But she wanted to catch up on what she'd missed. When she felt up to it, we turned off the TV and talked. Much of it was about the old days, when we moved into that house after my father died when I was in high school. He left us with no savings and no insurance, a surprise I think my mother never got over even though twelve years had passed since then.

Later, she would refer to it as a blessing in disguise. The almost empty accounts forced her to go back to school for the undergraduate degree she'd interrupted when I was born, and never finished. She'd always felt bad about being a quitter, and the diploma gave her a pride and a confidence I hadn't seen in her before. By the time she went on the market there was too much competition for the jobs she would have enjoyed, so she took an admin position and made herself indispensable enough to keep getting raises and respect from bosses who didn't want to lose her. In this way she paid for my own college, the mortgage on that house, our daily necessities, and the extras that made both of our lives better than they would have been otherwise.

I'd hoped that during this visit we could take a trip to the library, but she said she didn't feel up to it and asked me to pick out some books for her. I knew what she wanted: biographies of women who were still alive. Before she got sick, it didn't matter—she gobbled up histories of Emily Dickinson and Golda Meir, Joan of Arc, Cleopatra even—but now *still alive* was a prerequisite, for whatever reason she herself might or might not be aware; I was afraid to ask.

And if the woman had written her own book, all the better. I came back with a few for my mother to choose from. She started with the autobiography of Sonia Sotomayor, but set it aside after a few pages.

"It's not good?" I asked. "Or are you too tired?"

She shook her head. "Neither. I like it."

"Then why—?" I gestured at the book, where she'd marked her place with her hospital bracelet.

My mother sighed. "It used to inspire me, reading about women who've done things. Now it just makes me feel sad."

Another question I didn't want to ask. I didn't have to. She put her head back and fell asleep.

While she dozed, I picked up my notebook and did my best to write a few lines about the boy on the skateboard, but my heart wasn't in it, and the lines didn't lead anywhere. I'd thought that maybe I could come up with a little anecdote to read to her before I left, something like those early sketches of Chekhov's about strangers crossing paths and civil servants who misunderstand each other in amusing or poignant ways.

But really, I couldn't imagine anyone who might interest me less than the boy who came to water the plants while the next-door neighbors were away.

My mother woke with a start and asked, "Who are all these people?"

I said "*What?*" I wanted to ask if she'd been dreaming, but then I realized it wasn't a dream.

She said, "Oh. Sorry. Listen, Tess, I want to know what you think about something. Why are people so awful to each other now? So mean-spirited? What is it that's happened to us all?"

Her question threw me, I admit. It made *me* sad, contemplating an answer. "I should start dinner," I said instead. "While I'm doing that, why don't you think about the boy on the skateboard, and give me something to work with? We can collaborate."

"I'm not a fiction writer," she said, but I told her it didn't matter—you don't need to be a fiction writer to imagine someone else's life.

Over our spaghetti and meatballs, she asked about my real work, the collection of stories I was writing. I told her I'd hit a wall, a dead spot; it was hard for me to feel motivated, because I'd lost sight of what excited me about it in the first place. And with so much going on in the world, who cared? Was anybody actually reading anymore?

Now she was the one who sidestepped the question. "You'll get it back," she said. She'd been like this from the beginning, since I was a kid, encouraging me in my writing even though there's hardly any money in it and also no security, unless you happen to luck into the kind of teaching position I hoped to have someday. I knew other people whose parents had either squashed the creativity right out of them or barely tolerated it, all but insisting—if not outright insisting—that they go into something "sustainable" instead.

If there was any money at all in writing fiction, it lay in novels, not stories, but stories were all I wanted to write. In middle school I'd been a good sprinter, but never managed to finish the cross-country course. A writer I admire says that novels are like a lingering illness you might never get over, while stories are a blow to the solar plexus. I wanted to deliver that blow.

"I don't understand how you can be so supportive," I said to my mother, not for the first time. "Considering how unstable it all is. How unpredictable. And after Dad—"

"This doesn't have anything to do with Dad." She took a sip of milk to wash down her second meatball, winced a little swallowing, then set down her glass and fork. "It's what you want to do. You're good at it. You work hard. You'll be fine." Another labored swallow. "Besides, *I* love reading your stories. They always make me feel something. And they let me be somebody else for a while."

I blushed. I was thinking *Where would I be without my mother?*

"Just write from the heart," she added, and I felt a stab of pity because, as she herself had just said, she wasn't a fiction writer and didn't know how it was done. All the things you have to take into account, like what narrative perspective to write from and what stereotypes to avoid. How tricky it is not to cross the line into sentimentality, or even to know where that line is, and how hard to be as subtle as readers believe they want you to be.

After she said she couldn't eat any more spaghetti, I brought the dishes to the sink and made us sundaes, cutting up a banana and splitting it between the two bowls. I intended to pour caramel sauce only over her ice cream, but at the last minute I dribbled some on top of my own, too.

Before I could bring the bowls to the table, I heard a knock at the door. It was the boy on the skateboard, only now he tucked it tight to his side in such a natural way that it might have been a third arm. In his other hand he clutched a brown paper bag, which he held out to me. "Their cukes came up," he said, using his head to gesture at the house next door where he'd been tending the garden. "Nobody likes them at my house, so I thought I'd bring them over here."

"Oh, that's really nice of you," I said. I knew that in the other room, my mother would be interested in the conversation she could hear me having, and curious about who I was having it with, but I also knew she would probably not make the effort to get up from the table to come and find out.

Once, I was sitting alone on a bench in Madrid, where I spent a semester of my junior year because my mother insisted. "You can't say no to an opportunity like this," she said. "Trust me, if you do, they stop coming." Across from me on their own bench sat a mother with a daughter about my age. They'd caught my eye because I was feeling homesick. A boy gliding by on a skateboard caught sight of them, braked so abruptly he almost fell, laughed at himself, and ran over to have a brief but lively exchange with the girl. After they finished and he'd pushed off again, the mother leaned close and whispered, "Who was *that?*" I knew exactly what it was she asked, even though I couldn't hear it and didn't understand Spanish very well. I remember thinking that no one in the world would have been a fraction as interested as the girl's mother in who the boy had been. Recognizing this, I felt pierced by my homesickness, and by a premonition of the grief I would feel someday when my mother died. It was the first time I understood that the anticipation of grief is grief itself.

I took the cucumbers and thanked the boy, but he didn't turn to leave. "I saw you guys walking out there," he said, lowering his voice and nodding toward our driveway, where I'd taken my mother for her twice-a-day exercise. "She okay?"

It was only then that I saw he'd brushed the hair away from his face before knocking on our door. He might even have made an effort to smooth it. It was only then that I really bothered to focus on his face, and on the softness—a kind of fear almost, though not for himself—in eyes I had previously registered only as being dark.

"We're not sure yet," I told him. "But thanks for asking."

He nodded again, and there may have been a small smile, too. He didn't turn away then, either. "I noticed you have some crabgrass out there," he said, pointing to my mother's backyard, which had been left during the past few months to do whatever it wanted. "It'll die with the first frost, but in the spring it might come back and do a number on your lawn. I could come by and treat it now so that doesn't happen, if you want. It wouldn't take too much, if you wanted me to."

I thanked him a third time and asked for his name—Roscoe Platz—and his phone number. Returning to the table with our dessert, I described the encounter to my mother. "Enterprising young man," she said. I asked if she could eat a little more of her sundae, but she shook her head. "Maybe he's saving up for college. Sure, I'll call him. I haven't liked the looks of things out there myself—I've let it get out of hand."

Roscoe Platz ended up coming to our house the next day and treating the grass, but that isn't the point of the story. The point of the story is that when I returned to my apartment on Sunday night, I ate dinner with my roommate and then instead of watching a movie with her, I said I thought I would do some work instead. I told myself when I sat down that I would write something just for my mother—something no one else would have to see—and this made it easier, the words came almost before I could catch them, and I wrote an entire draft before going to bed. The title I gave it was "Where Has All the Kindness Gone?" after the folk song about flowers and soldiers, which my mother sang to me when I was little because her own mother had sung it to *her*. I knew the title was what my students would call cheesy, but I took a chance, and the next day I polished the story and sent it out. To my shock it ended up in a magazine I'd thought was too high to aim for, and then an editor asked if I had any other stories and she took my collection, and after it was published it won a prize, after which I applied for a full-time teaching job and got it.

Where would I be without my mother? I found out too soon, before I was ready. But then, is anyone ever?

Ride Share

I gave myself the assignment of finding out if there's a God. I didn't think it would be that hard. Of course I know it's a question philosophers and regular people have been asking forever. But I wasn't trying to prove anything or persuade anyone. I only wanted to find out if there was a God for *me*.

How to go about such a thing, though? I tried churches, different ones, but ended up every Sunday wishing the sermon would end soon and thinking about the groceries I'd buy on the way home. I tried sitting in nature and listening for a voice, but all I heard were birds. I liked those sounds, but if they came from God it was indirectly, and I couldn't tell what they might mean. I tried meditating but fell asleep.

On my work computer one day an ad popped up, asking if I might be interested in an "explorers' retreat" offered at a spiritual center on the South Shore. I figured they'd targeted me because of my research online about churches. That gave me a weird feeling—realizing that a spiritual center must have hired a search optimization service—but then I figured, why should they be different from any other business? I didn't fool myself that they'd contacted me because of an interest in improving or saving my soul. Or at least, not because of that mostly or only. They charged a fee, after all.

And why shouldn't they, if they were going to provide something as valuable as a path to God?

So I decided not to hold it against them, and clicked on the website. From where I was sitting, it looked pretty good. The retreat center appeared to be something of a castle (there had been actual castles in New England?), situated on lush green land between a forest and a lake. If you'd asked me to describe a place that looked "spiritual," I couldn't have done a better job than to direct you to the photos on that site.

It didn't have a name other than "The Center." At first this seemed odd, until I remembered that not far from where I lived there was a country club called "The Country Club." Isn't simplicity what we're all supposed to be striving for?

If you signed up to be an explorer at The Center, you didn't have to share a room with anyone (that would have been a deal-breaker for me, but to be honest that's a big part of why I was looking for God, because I was so afraid of other people); you even got a private bath. There were spots available in a session beginning at the end of the month, and I happened to be in the position of needing to use a week's vacation or losing it.

A sign? From who—God, already? How would I know, one way or the other?

Since that was the whole point, I filled in my name, address, and the session I wanted to register for. When the form for payment came up, I hesitated—I mean, I wasn't born yesterday. It was then I noticed a link labeled *Explorer Endorsements* and clicked on it. My screen filled with dozens of phrases like "life-changing"; "monumental"; and my favorite, "shook me to the core in the best possible way," along with enough negative ones ("food could be better"; "my room was too cold") that I entered my credit card number before I could lose my nerve and back out the way I always did with things that at first seemed like things I wanted to do, but then became too scary.

I sat at my desk and tried to regulate my breathing the way my meditation app advised, but before I could do so, my inbox pinged with an email congratulating me on the step I'd just taken to satisfy my spiritual hunger. It was obviously a form letter, but I liked its tone—warm and welcoming. The signature was *Your Fellow Pilgrim, Bodhi Chaudhury.*

An Indian guy. That made sense. I formed an immediate image: around my own age or a little older (thirty, say), ponytail, chill. Someone who would look at the person beneath the surface, to the things that really mattered. I looked up the name *Bodhi* and found that it meant "awakening, enlightenment." I imagined he'd trained in India with the masters and then come to the U.S. to spread the word.

There were attachments for me to fill out and return—dietary preferences, a medical waiver, questions about physical limitations. They were sorry but they could not accommodate pets, though of course service and emotional support animals were allowed.

What would it take to prove that Stella was an emotional support cat? But no, I told myself. The whole point was to find something new to count on, and different. Probably something inside myself.

The final document they asked for was something called a Spiritual Inventory, with questions about previous religious affiliations, childhood places of worship, and any inclinations I might have toward a specific set of beliefs. I was going to leave it blank or write that the whole point for me was that I *had* no history or inclinations, but then I worried that these responses could have been perceived as either negligent or hostile.

So instead I typed, "I heard someone say once that God is like the wind. You can't see it, but you know it's there because you can see how it moves what it passes through, like hair and tree branches. I guess you could say I'm looking for a God-wind."

God-wind. That was poetic of me, I thought. Possibly even profound. I enjoyed a vision of some office assistant plucking my registration out of the pile and placing it in a special folder Bodhi would want to take a look at before all of us explorers arrived.

I thought that would be the end of things before I arrived for my session (if I didn't chicken out, which was a big if). But as I sat there wondering what I'd gotten myself into, in chimed another email. "What you wrote about a God-wind is beautiful, Gabby," Bodhi Chaudhury had written. "I look forward to accompanying you on your spiritual quest."

I knew he intended this to be the end of our correspondence, but I couldn't help myself. I replied to his note, thanking him for taking the time to give me individual attention when I knew he must be very busy at The Center.

"It's my pleasure," he wrote back; this time I'd half-hoped, half-waited for the ping. Before signing off again he added, "If you care to tell me any details about yourself that might help me understand what you hope to accomplish in your time with us, feel free to write me at my personal email" and he included the address.

I thanked him for the invitation and wrote that though it wasn't easy for me to take a leap of faith like this, he'd already convinced me of its rightness. I told him I wasn't used to confiding in anyone, especially about the habits and impulses I wished I could learn to control. Before I sent the note, I erased the words "unhealthy" and "destructive" before "habits" and "impulses"—I figured he didn't need all the gory details.

I think everyone has those, Bodhi responded. *I know I do. What would you say if I told you that before I began praying every day for the compulsion to be removed, I used to be so worried I might hurt someone that whenever I was around people I kept my hands clasped behind my back? I mean everywhere, all the time. Work. Family gatherings. You can imagine how awkward that was.*

Wow. I sat back to take that in. How would you go grocery shopping, or eat? And did that mean he was single, or had been, back when he suffered in this way? I thought about asking these and other questions, but before I could decide whether that was too nosy, he popped in to continue.

But trust me—it is possible to change and, even more important, to forgive ourselves. All things are possible with God.

That last line lifted me out of my seat. Literally: I stood up from my desk feeling lighter than I could remember since before high school. Before middle school, even. I'd never told anyone the things I'd just written to Bodhi, and he congratulated me for getting a head start on my journey. I know "journey" is the word everybody uses, about everything, but somehow from Bodhi it didn't seem trite.

When people at work asked what I was going to do with my time off, I said I planned a staycation. I knew they didn't really care; they were only asking to be polite. "That sounds nice," they said. "Enjoy some downtime." The only person I told the truth to was my brother, in our weekly video call, after I'd spoken to my niece and nephew who always asked me to hold Stella up to the screen because they wanted a cat but their mother was allergic.

Usually, my brother and I only exchanged a few words at the beginning and end of the call. I considered him basically the tech guy who facilitated my visits with Max and Lilly.

I probably told James about the retreat because I figured he'd talk me out of it. I knew what *he* thought of God, and I figured he'd have something snarky to say about my efforts to track down something that didn't exist.

But he only listened without interrupting. Then he said, "Well, I hope you find what you're looking for, Gab."

What? What is happening?! I wanted to shout at the screen. *Why aren't you telling me I'm an idiot, that I'm wasting my money, that spirituality is just a New Age buzzword for people who can't figure out how to take charge of their own lives?* But I didn't say any of this, and he only added, "You've checked it out, right? You're sure it isn't a scam."

"Of course I did," I told him. "There were attachments and everything."

He said he looked forward to hearing about it afterward. He added, "Just remember, retreat means to go backwards," and I thought, *There* it is! *That* was the brother I knew.

On Sunday morning after breakfast, I stood in front of my bathroom mirror and looked into it longer than I usually let myself. A quote from *The Color Purple* was taped to the mirror ("I try to teach my heart not to want things it can't have"), but I didn't need to read it anymore, because of course I had it memorized. It was my mantra. I didn't look at the quote but at my face, for so long it began to blur—which was a relief.

Before I left the apartment, I took a quick trip to the tiny balcony outside my living room. The building called them "Juliet" balconies, but that was just marketing. We all had them—strip platforms big enough that you could keep a few plants out there, if you wanted. You weren't supposed to actually step out onto it (there was a rule, because of the weight limit), but sometimes people did, including me. I always told myself I wanted to get some fresh air or feel the sun on my face, but if you want to know the truth, it was superstition. I was tempting fate. My apartment was on the sixth floor, so if the balcony held me up, I was supposed to live that day. It was as simple as that.

And if it didn't, well—would that be so bad?

It was the beginning of May and green buds were everywhere. Hard not to feel hopeful.

Stella watched me warily as I stepped out on the balcony and waited for the worst. When it didn't happen, I came back in and picked up my suitcase, surprised to see my hands shaking.

My driver was scheduled for ten o'clock, but I stood ready in the foyer of my building at quarter to, because I was so excited to be on my way. I'd thought about taking the stairs down instead of the elevator, because for a while I tried that, but I didn't see a need to add any more stress to the morning than I already felt. *The next time I walk through that door*, I thought, *I will be a new person*. I couldn't wait.

I was expecting a man because the driver's name was Rene, but when the Sentra pulled up I saw that it was in fact a woman about my own age behind the wheel. She was dressed all in black, including one of those chauffeur caps you see on limo drivers in the movies. Was that a joke? It didn't seem so; she seemed to take the job pretty seriously. When she got out to help me put my bag in the trunk, I saw that she moved with a hitch, leading with her shoulder and dragging her body along behind it. It would be fair to say she scuttled rather than walked, in addition to which she was as short as a child.

So she was deformed, then. But who was I to judge? Maybe when I became more spiritual, I'd learn to accept more—in other people, and in myself—than I ever had before.

Rene asked if I wanted her to pull the front passenger seat forward so I'd have more room, but I told her I was fine and we took off. She said the GPS estimate for our drive was less than an hour. "Smart to travel on Sunday morning," she added, and I told her it hadn't been my choice, that I was headed to a kind of camp session that began at noon.

"Camp?" she said, in a curious tone, and I blushed and admitted that it was a spiritual retreat. I must have wanted her to know this, because her comment about it being smart to travel now hadn't required a response. And I was glad I did tell her, because at the words *spiritual retreat* she nodded and said "Got it," and in the rear-view I thought I saw an expression of approval and interest, which made me feel good even though she was a stranger.

Then she met my glance in the reflection, and I felt a flash of discomfort seeing those rabbit eyes that were too sharp for her small, round face. They were like black lasers homing in on a target. She smiled, but it didn't undo the effect, and I looked away. Too bad for her, I thought—her eyes and her funny way of moving must put people off.

I decided to stay quiet because I wanted to be in a thoughtful frame of mind when I arrived. Rene seemed to get this, too. She turned the volume down on her playlist and didn't speak again until we passed a sign indicating that we'd entered the town where The Center was located. "Two minutes," she said, and I sat up straighter, propelled by nervous excitement. "I think I see the castle," I said, as the levitating sensation returned. But then we passed what turned out to be an old brick water tower covered with *No Trespassing* signs.

Two minutes later, when the GPS told us we'd arrived at our destination, the address belonged to an abandoned storefront. No castle in sight. Rene murmured something from the front that I didn't hear, and I asked her to double-check.

I'm sure you already guessed where this was going. We drove around until we came to a little common, at which point Rene stopped the car, got out, and lurched toward an older couple walking their dog. The couple appeared on their guard as she approached, but she must have persuaded them that she wasn't a threat because they began smiling and allowed her to pet the dog. They said there had never been a retreat center—let alone a castle—in that town. Rene began reporting this when she came back to the car and I said, "It's okay, you don't need to tell me."

She thumped herself back against the driver's seat and gave me that pointy look of hers in the mirror. "They really got you," she said, and it was a few seconds before I realized she didn't mean that The Center (or, more specifically, Bodhi) had *understood* me. "Doesn't that make you mad?"

Was "mad" what I was feeling? Well, it might have been in there with all the other things.

I told Rene I just wanted to go home. She nodded and turned the car around. Our trip up the highway was as silent as the trip down until she said, "You're a good person, Gabby."

Was she angling for a better tip than I might give her otherwise? How would she know whether I was a good person or not? As I was trying to figure out whether I'd be even more of a chump than I already was to think anything different, she added, "You don't deserve what just happened to you."

I mumbled a cross between *Thanks* and *Shut up*. Mumbling was a trick my father taught me for when you're not sure what to say. *They'll think it's their fault they can't understand you*, he told me. *It gets you off the hook.*

My brother never bought into the mumbling, but I was a fan. James went the other way, always making sure he was clear about what he was thinking or feeling—*too* clear sometimes, if you ask me. Sometimes people are just as happy to leave things obscure.

Rene might have been one of them because she didn't ask me to repeat myself. "Maybe the bank will refund your money," she said. "If you explain what they did to you."

"It was a couple of weeks ago," I told her. "Besides, I don't care." It was true. I was stupid, stupid, stupid. Didn't somebody as stupid as I was deserve to pay a price?

The money was one thing. But what was more on my mind was Bodhi's story about being so afraid of hurting someone that he always kept his hands clenched behind his back. Why had he told me that? I'd already signed up. They'd already charged my card. So was it just for sick kicks, or could this compulsion have been something Bodhi himself—or, rather, the scammer pretending to be an Indian guy named Bodhi—had suffered?

No, I decided. It had just been a tactic to seal the deal, a detail stolen from some other sap who'd responded to an email inviting him (*her?*) to confess a torment.

My eyes stung and I thought I might puke. I put my sunglasses on and swallowed, to keep from letting the scammers win.

There were more cars on the highway than on our first leg of the trip, but it still wasn't bad. I wished for a traffic jam, or a complete standstill and hours-long road closure because of an accident bad enough to require many emergency vehicles without causing a death.

But no—we just sailed along until we came to my exit. At the end of the ramp, Rene had trouble entering a long line of cars. She kept trying to signal the other drivers to let her in, and they kept ignoring her. Eventually she pushed her way in, and I saw her gesture at the black Audi that blasted its horn behind us. We began inching forward. "Oh, shit," she said. "I think I just crashed a funeral procession. Not only that, I gave them the finger."

Sure enough, I looked out to see the headlights lit on all the cars around us, with little flags front and back. "It's okay with me," I said. "You can just stay here. I'm in no hurry."

In the mirror I saw Rene's surprised then reproachful look. "You're not serious, right? For one thing, it's illegal. It's also morally wrong. These people are grieving, Gabby."

"No shit," I said. Did she think she was telling me something I didn't already know? It was fine with me to be surrounded by sad people. It was where I belonged.

She tried frantically to catch the attention of the driver behind her—the one she'd established a relationship with. I could tell she wanted to apologize, and I wondered how she planned to accomplish this. In the end it didn't work; she had to make the turn leading to my street without managing to express her regret at having flipped off the mourners.

I saw that it bothered her, a lot. I considered saying something about how anybody could make that mistake, but I figured it wouldn't mean anything coming from a chump like me.

Before I was ready, we pulled up in front of my building. When I didn't make a move to get out, I knew Rene understood that if I went back right then to my apartment with only the cat waiting for me, I would die myself, at least in some ways.

It was clear she still felt bad about disrespecting the cortege. "You know what?" She eased the Sentra forward into a Visitor spot. "I should check the app and see if I have to go anywhere. Just give me a sec."

While she thumbed through her phone screen I sat and tried to regulate my breathing, and reminded myself of how much Stella loved me. Then Rene put the phone down and told me she was good, nobody needed her. "You want to take a walk or something? Get some lunch?"

I shook my head. I'd decided to just remain in the car and see what happened. I supposed she could call the police if she wanted, and have them remove me. But the next thing I knew, I'd opened the door and stepped onto the pavement.

Has that ever happened to you, or *for* you? You make a decision not to do something—and feel good about it, or at least relieved the decision's been made—and then you find yourself doing the very thing you just decided not to?

Rene was still wearing the silly chauffeur's cap as she came around to the trunk and popped it open, then lifted out my bag. "It's really pretty around here," she said. "Where I live there's no—"

"Am I the fattest person you ever met?"

This was something I hadn't intended, either; it just came out. She seemed more surprised by the interruption than by the question itself. "No," she said without hesitating. "Maybe the *second* biggest."

That she hadn't used my own word for it made me feel like crying, but only for an instant before I shut it down. I didn't ask who the first biggest was, though I would have loved to hear.

I grabbed my bag from her and said, "That hat of yours is ridiculous, you know. It makes you look like a gnome."

She almost smiled. Was that what it was? "I do know," she said. "My father gave it to me. He's always telling me I should 'dress the part'—he thinks it'll make a difference in how people see me. But I'm like, *Dad*, a spaz wearing a chauffeur's cap is still a spaz."

"You're not a spaz," I said. It was an automatic response, and I knew she could tell I didn't mean it. "Why do you wear it then?" I asked, to cover my insincerity.

She shrugged. "He loves me. And what do I know? Maybe he's right." But she took the cap off and tossed it onto the passenger seat. "Look, Gabby, I'm going to park here for a while and take myself off the app. If you get up there and feel like talking or anything, just call me or come back down."

"You don't have to do that," I said. "In fact, you shouldn't. The Visitor spots are for—"

"I know. I'm visiting." She waved off my protest. "You have my number. I'll be here."

I gave another mumble and turned away, so I didn't have to look at her strange body or her strange eyes anymore. As I entered my building I remembered thinking, only a few hours earlier, that I'd return as a new person. What a joke!

My next-door neighbor was just leaving her unit as I approached my own. As far as I knew all she ever did was go to the gym and work out, but I was tempted to like her anyway. "Oh, hi, Abby," she said, catching sight of my suitcase. "Going somewhere?"

That morning I'd heard her call to someone inside her own unit, "Holy shit. She's out on her fatio" when I stepped onto my Juliet balcony.

At least, I *think* that's what she said. She might have said "patio," in which case, was it possible she'd been afraid for me?

There was no way of knowing. But I couldn't take that chance. I told her no, I wasn't going anywhere, in fact I was coming back.

Stella didn't run to greet me, as I'd expected she would; she only blinked when I entered the bedroom and let my suitcase fall over on the floor. Well, no wonder! I saw she'd already eaten all the food I'd left out, which was supposed to last the whole day.

I opened the window and stuck my arm out, waiting for a breeze. Since I'd left that morning, things had turned warmer and greener. I looked down to see Rene's car still there, the chauffeur's cap on the seat beside her. "Freak," I whispered, but I added her phone number to my Contacts list because you never know, it might come in handy to have a driver's personal number if you really need it someday.

Stella was too interested in the sounds and smells from outside, so I shut the window and looked at the clock to see that after all this, it was still only noon. Since it was the regular time for the video call with my brother, I texted and he wrote back, "I thought you were at your thing???"

"Change of plans," I replied, and a few minutes later we were onscreen together. I could hear the kids screeching somewhere in the house behind him.

I told James he'd been right—it had all been a scam. I waited for him to remind me he'd told me so. But instead he said, "I'm really sorry, Gab. Does this mean you're going to give up... looking?"

It almost sounded like hope, what I heard in his voice, but I couldn't tell what for. I said it was all bullshit, and people sucked. I asked him to put the kids on. They were slower than usual to appear on the screen, and during that time my brother and I asked each other how we were, and we both said we were good, and then I asked him how his work was going, but before he could give an answer, my niece showed up to save us. "Where's Stella?" she asked.

"She's too fat to move right now," I told her. "Stella's a pig. A pathetic excuse for a cat. A disgusting—"

"Hey." James interrupted in his annoyingly gentle voice. "The kids are planning a show for you, but I don't think it's ready yet."

"Oh, that's sweet." I smiled to show I'd only been kidding, calling Stella those names. "Comedy? Tragedy? Can I have a hint?"

"It's about the apocalypse," Lilly said, and Max added, "No survivors!"

"So, a comedy," I said, but they didn't laugh.

Their mother called them from the background and the kids ran off, and it was just me and my brother again. "Please don't give up, Gabby," he said. He lifted his hand toward his camera and for a moment my screen was covered by the curtain of his palm. I thought he was trying to block me from seeing whatever was on his end.

Then his arm extended through my computer, into my bedroom and across my desk, reaching for my hand. I shrieked and tried to jerk it back as Stella dropped from the bed and bolted, but my brother's grip was too strong, and he had me.

I yelled, "What are you doing?"

But I already knew. He was doing what he'd done all his life, since we were little. Back then it wasn't his own idea—our mother made him. "Hold your sister's hand": how often had I heard her say that over the years? It was me who used to lace our fingers together; he would have just mitted my fist like a ball if he had the choice. Whenever we got where we were going, he'd let go not just by dropping my hand, but by pushing it down and away from him—almost like a dance move, only not—to make it clear it wasn't a job he wanted.

Back then, it made sense. We lived in the same house and went to the same school, and he could actually do something if I was in trouble: scare off a persecutor, or set me straight if I wandered off in the wrong direction.

Now we sat at our separate desks in our separate homes in our separate states, connected only by cables. Somehow James had found a way to breach all the barriers, and touch me. His hand felt warm and tight, not loose and sweaty like the old days. "Don't give up," he repeated. "Gabby—I'm begging you."

Was Rene close enough to hear if I screamed for help? Was anyone?

Instead of screaming I asked, "How is this possible?" I didn't recognize my own voice anymore. "How did you figure this out?"

My brother squeezed harder. Soon I'd have to tell him to let go a little, because it hurt. He smiled uncertainly, as if he didn't know whether I'd asked a real question or not. He said, "Come on. What are you talking about? You know how."

I was afraid to tell him I didn't understand. Maybe this was a thing now and I'd missed it. Maybe to him and everybody else it was no big deal—not a miracle, the way it was to me.

An Early Departure

It wasn't the best time for me to be out of the office, but my niece asked so of course I went. The train ride to New York took four hours. For quite a few years when my niece was little, we used to meet up there, all of us, on a Saturday in autumn—my sister and her two children, my mother and me—arriving from different places by train and having a hectic stand-up lunch at Penn Station before checking into our hotel. We'd go to a show, eat at John's Pizzeria afterward, then walk through Times Square with us grown-ups flanking the kids, though looking back I wonder how much protection we could have provided if anyone really wanted to get at them; we were only three women, with not that much weight among us. Still, we would have had the advantage of our investment in the children's safety, which counts for a lot.

My sister and I look alike, and my niece looks like both of us, and I knew that anyone seeing me hold Tanya's hand back then as we strolled down the street might easily take me for her mother. I savored this more than I should have, but I figured it didn't hurt anyone; nobody else had to know.

Before bedtime on those Saturday nights, we hung out together in one of the hotel rooms, just catching up and watching the kids goof around. One year, my sister booked a hotel with a rooftop pool, and how much fun was *that!* Watching my niece and nephew laugh and splash under the stars. Another year we arranged the trip around my fortieth birthday, and they sang to me over a red-velvet cake from Magnolia Bakery. I got the impression that they all made a special effort to give me a nice time, knowing how I might feel turning forty with no children of my own. Nobody said this out loud, but they were right that I felt a certain way, and the celebration helped in the moment even though it made me sadder when I was alone on the train back to Boston the next day.

Back then I liked to read quotes from successful women about not having children. Like Jennifer Aniston, who said, "You may not have a child come out of your vagina, but that doesn't mean you aren't mothering." *I'm mothering*, I told myself, whenever I spent time with my sister's kids. *So what if they didn't come out of my vagina. Is that such a big deal?*

On Sunday mornings of those weekends, we ate brunch together before we all headed back to Penn Station for our rides home on three different tracks. They were short visits, sometimes not even a whole twenty-four hours, but they were the most alive and comforting times I can remember—the kids so captivated by the novelties they saw around them (pretzels the size of their faces, horse buggies in Central Park), and so eager to join the scene. The year my nephew Henry was nine, I bought him a stuffed frog from a street vendor, and Henry promptly named the frog Hoppy, placed it on his head, and proceeded to walk around that way the entire day. My mother was healthy enough to walk long distances with us, from the park all the way down Fifth Avenue to where we always stayed near Rockefeller Center.

Tanya works there now, apprenticing to writers for a comedy sketch show. It's her dream job, straight out of college, the one she'd told us she wanted when she was eleven and we all took the NBC backstage tour. The others of us smiled and said *of course* she would get a job like that, though none of us really believed it.

But we should never have doubted her. Once when she was three, we went to a minor-league baseball game, and our seats were across the stadium from a pop-up carnival. Tanya caught sight of the Ferris wheel, pointed to let us know she was headed there, and took off. My sister and I followed the whole way, keeping her safe without her knowing, and we were amused but more than a little unsettled when the baby never looked back.

TANYA ASKED ME TO COME SEE HER IN THE CITY, and followed this up with a second request, which was not to tell her mother. This was tricky, because she wouldn't say why, but I convinced myself it had something to do with wanting to surprise her mother somehow. My sister's birthday wasn't for another six months, and it wasn't a big one, but in this way I allowed myself to honor Tanya's request, and to book my train tickets without mentioning it to my sister in our every-other-day text exchange. Why Tanya herself didn't just tell me whatever she needed to in a text or email, I couldn't guess, though it would become clear all too soon why she wanted to see me in person.

My niece apologized for not being able to put me up, but of course I understood—this was New York! She shared a two-bedroom walk-up with two friends from college; one of them paid a little less and slept in the dining alcove. I remembered such arrangements from being young myself, though in Boston, not New York. When I got older I would never have wanted to live in the same circumstances, but at the time, it was fun.

Besides, I could afford a nice hotel room. I checked in early, then met Tanya at one of the subterranean restaurants at 30 Rock. It was January, and from our table we watched the skaters on the rink outside. I hadn't seen her in half a year, since we'd all gotten together in the place my mother lived to celebrate *her* big birthday, but I was glad to see that my niece hadn't changed much since then. One of my favorite things about her had always been her sweetness, and I admit that when she first told me she was moving there, I was afraid the city might turn her hard.

"How's Grandma?" she asked. "I wish she could still make the trip down here. But she seems to be doing better than a lot of people her age."

I agreed, and kept myself from reminding her that she could always inquire of Grandma herself how Grandma was doing. I didn't want to start off on a rocky foot.

I'd speculated a lot, of course, about why Tanya had asked me to make the trip down. Did she need money, and hesitated to ask her parents? Had something happened she didn't want them to know about? Was she pregnant and sought my advice?

I can't deny it made me feel special to have been summoned. My niece said she needed me, so I dropped everything and went.

"It's about Henry," she said, after the server had left the table. I knew she'd ordered the least expensive item on the menu because she expected me to insist on paying, which I would. "He's in trouble."

"What kind?" In the moment before concern hit, I felt surprise. Her brother, a senior in college, had always been a quiet kid, not afraid to go his own way but not interested in ruffling any feathers, either. At least, that's how it always seemed to me. It was hard to tell, because of the quietness. He spent a lot of time on his computer—to the extent that I knew my sister sometimes worried about his eyes—but he seemed to enjoy our family visits, never hiding in his room or otherwise retreating when we were all together. I couldn't imagine what sort of trouble my niece might be talking about.

He'd gotten himself involved in a hacking scheme, Tanya told me. There were plenty of kids at his school who knew how proficient he was at finding his way around various systems, and plenty who needed their grades boosted and would pay to have it done.

Slowly, I repeated Tanya's words aloud: *gotten himself involved*. "You make it sound as if he couldn't help it. As if he had no choice." I noticed that my hand was trembling as I reached for my water glass. Tanya saw it, too. "And I wouldn't call that 'getting in trouble'—I'd call it committing a crime."

She sucked her breath in, barely audibly, and sat back in her chair. "I didn't expect you to be so harsh," she said. "This is *Henry* we're talking about."

"I know." It chilled me to see the look of distrust in her eyes. "You think I'm not worried?"

And then through the sense-channel that connects women in a family, our mutual mind's eye, I could see we were both remembering the day her brother walked around New York with his new favorite stuffie balanced on top of his head. Oh, Hoppy! I put a hand to my throat.

She leaned closer, and I could see she was wearing the butterfly necklace I'd given her on her sixteenth birthday. My immediate response was to feel flattered, but this was followed by a flash of insight I wished I could ignore: she'd worn the necklace to butter me up. "It's not like he *meant* to commit a crime," she said.

Somehow, I managed not to exclaim. How delusional was she? How willing to ignore what she knew—never mind common sense—in order to believe, instead, what she wished to be true? "Yaya," I said, then waited for her to look directly at me. "Hacking into somebody else's database and changing the numbers—he had to understand that's a criminal act."

"No, I *know,*" she said, not bothering to hide her irritation, "but it didn't start out like that." She went on to recount the story of a crush her brother had, on a girl who seemed to like him back. "But it turned out she only made nice so he'd change her Civics grade." I could tell how hurt Tanya had been to hear this, on her brother's behalf. And I remembered the kick it had always given me to hear her use old-timey phrases such as *made nice*.

"So she dumped him afterward?" I asked. "What made her think he wouldn't just go into the system again and change the grade back?"

"Because," she said, "she knew him enough to tell what kind of guy he is."

"So where does it stand? Did somebody expose him, is there an investigation?"

Tanya nodded. "The college's disciplinary board. He's afraid he's going to be expelled. And after that, the dean said, they might involve the police."

"He hasn't told your parents?"

"No. And he doesn't want them to find out."

The server came and put our lunches in front of us. Neither of us reached for a fork. "Why are you telling *me*, then?" I asked, though of course I already knew.

It chilled me again to see how much, in that moment, she hated me for making her say it. "We thought… because of your job… you might be able to…" But she couldn't finish. Instead she dropped her face toward her chest and began to sob. "I'm sorry, Aunt Kim, I should never have asked you. I know it's shitty, I know it's wrong, and trust me, Henry does, too. But he begged me. He didn't think you would do it if *he* asked, but he knows you're like a second mother to me."

Ah, those magic words: "a second mother." They are meant to be a compliment—one of the highest—but the person they are addressed to, the person so named, understands all too well how far the second mother falls short of the first.

My sister had often referred to me as a second mother in relation to her own children, especially Tanya. I knew she meant well and wanted to make me feel good. And I would have felt touched by my niece using the phrase now, except that I realized she was doing so in an effort to get what she and her brother wanted.

So she had become a little hard, after all. I knew she would not have relished this task of trying to secure my help, but she had her priorities in order, and her brother came first. I had to admire it. She was still the girl who set out for her destination with no intention of letting anyone stop her along the way.

"I'm sorry, Yaya," I told her (and there was a considerable part of me that *was* sorry, the part that should have done what any mother would do), "but I really can't intervene. Not that I think it would help any, even if I did."

"Of course it would. They'd listen to you." She was pleading. I saw that her eyes were dry, and a soundless crash in my ribcage told me her sobbing had been fake.

Realizing I had to find a way to steel myself, I pretended I was speaking to a client, instead of my beloved niece. I told her that matters like these had nothing to do with the ones I dealt with in my job. Even if the college did contact the police and press charges, my reach—my jurisdiction in a different kind of agency, and a different state—wouldn't come close.

But it wasn't only that it wouldn't work or that I might get exposed, I told her. It would be the wrong thing to do. That I had to say this made me feel like crying myself, and the truth was that I said it even before I'd finished mentally running through the sequence of people I might conceivably call to make life easier on my nephew.

"I know it doesn't seem like it right now," I said, "but even if I did try to help, it wouldn't be the best thing for Henry."

"Why not? He's learned his lesson. He'll never do anything like this again."

"But he did it *this* time. And it wasn't a momentary lapse of judgment—that kind of thing has to be thought out. It has to be planned. It's better for him to face the consequences, in the long run. Trust me."

She had zero intention of trusting me; this I could see in her face. "So you're not even going to try?" Her eyes pricked like points of glass.

"Oh, Yaya." In that moment I understood that the most rewarding aspect of my existence, the role that had sustained and buoyed me for more than twenty years in an otherwise lonely life, had just come to its end. "I can't."

Before I arrived, I'd hoped she'd bring me back to her office and show me around—she'd mentioned something, on the phone when we made arrangements, to this effect—but it became clear after I paid the check, after we took the escalator back up to the lobby, that she intended for us to part ways. I hugged her, I hugged her, not wanting to let go even though I knew she'd already slipped away from me to a place I'd not be allowed to enter, if I ever managed to find it again.

I'd booked the hotel room for that night expecting that Tanya would let me treat her and her friends to a dinner they wouldn't have been able to afford on their own. I confess I had fantasies about how proud she'd feel of her cool and generous aunt, and the way all the girls would hug and thank me when we stepped out of the restaurant.

But now I didn't need the room, on top of which I wanted only to get away from the city. I canceled at the hotel even though it was too late to get a refund, then took a cab to Penn Station where I changed my return ticket, which cost me a fee. But it was worth it; Amtrak would not be able to hurtle me home fast enough.

Home? Well, no. But back to where I belonged.

On the ride to Boston I sat on the side that gave a view of the water, when there was water to see. In New London, a young mother got on with a boy who was about two years old and miserable, crying not for any particular reason but for the sake of crying; it's easy to tell the difference, if you've spent any time around kids. I helped her collapse his stroller, and offered him the bag of crackers I'd bought at the station but not yet opened. The mother fell all over herself thanking me, and the crackers distracted him for a while, but when the bag was empty he threw it on the floor and started crying again.

I couldn't change my seat, not only because the train was full but also because the mother would know why I moved, and I didn't want to make her feel bad. I pulled out a folder and tried to look at some work, but it was futile. Partly this was because of the boy's whining, but mainly it had to do with how sick I felt about the scene I'd just had with my niece.

At one point I sighed and let my glance fall across the aisle. The mother seemed to take this as an invitation. She leaned over and whispered, "It gets easier, right?" in a tone that attempted lightness but couldn't conceal the desperation it contained.

I understood instantly what she assumed about me, and perceived the familiar, shameful thrill of passing. "You'll be *amazed*," I said, and something about the way I pronounced the word must have intrigued the boy or tickled him (the buzzy *Z* sound!) because he paused in his crying to look up at me and smile. I smiled back. The mother jumped on it, grabbing first one toy and then another out of the diaper bag at her feet, and these distractions finally took hold. Her son became immersed in a handheld pinball game and stayed quiet for the rest of their ride.

I felt a wave of pride I knew to be ridiculous, but it blunted the despair I'd boarded with. Only later, pulling into my station after they'd gotten off a few stops before, did the truth set in. Clutching my workbag tighter than necessary as I stepped onto the platform, I realized that of course I hadn't fooled the boy as I had his mother. Didn't I understand children better than that? He'd smiled at me not because I'd charmed him, but to let me know he recognized a liar when he saw one. Jennifer Aniston could pretend all she wanted, but this kid wasn't about to let me get away with offering a promise that wasn't mine to make.

First Day

This morning, the person in the car ahead of me at the drive-thru bought me my coffee.

When I rolled up to the window, the cashier said, "Already taken care of" and pointed at the Civic turning out of the lot. "You want a donut or something too? She gave me her card and said to put on whatever."

I was flustered, I admit; it was so unexpected. I said just the coffee would be fine, and then I kept thanking her, as if she was the one who'd made the gesture. After I took the cup and moved up, I realized that I was supposed to have given my card to the cashier and paid for the person behind *me*. But by then it was too late. Instead of feeling grateful to the Civic driver, I felt guilty.

Why do these things keep happening to me? It's not because I'm unwilling to do my part. I just somehow never manage to catch on or catch up in time, and then I feel bad.

On the other hand, this business of paying it forward and committing random acts of kindness strikes me as silly and kind of dumb. I don't know, I'm suspicious of it. It seems like a recipe for feeling good about yourself without really having to do much of anything. Another gimmick to post about. Just leave me out of it!

I have—I had—the most boring job on the planet, but I tried not to let it get me down. Well, maybe not the *most* boring. I dated a guy once who'd spent his teenage summers lying on his stomach in the back of a tractor, reaching down to pick cucumbers as the truck drove through the field. Two hours going one way, then two hours down a different row in the other direction. Then lunch, then another round to make for an eight-hour shift. There were a dozen kids doing the same thing all around him on the flatbed, picking up cukes and tossing them into buckets. When they came upon bad ones, they threw them at each other—not hard, not to hurt, but just for something to do that wasn't the job. When I heard this story, I thought, *Damn*. I would never have had that in me. But the guy I dated talked about it with cheer, and even said it had been fun sometimes. "We were kids," he reminded me. "'Bored' wasn't a thing." We broke up soon after that, probably because I knew he was such a better person than me.

The first day of spring had come and gone, and it was still gray and no warmer than the winter. Clouds were predicted all week. The general feeling in the air was one of gloom. When I got to work, I wished I'd thought to get some donuts to put in the break room, though whether I would have let the woman in the Civic pay for them I couldn't say, since it didn't occur to me until too late. Everyone seemed to be in an extra bad mood, and before long I found out why: the company was being sold, and a bunch of us were about to lose our jobs. *Ooh, ooh, pick me!* I thought, even as I recognized that it was not what I was supposed to hope for. When my boss called me in and told me how sorry she was, that I'd get two weeks of severance, that I'd have her highest recommendation wherever I applied next, etc., it was all I could do to pretend to feel upset.

I was sprung, suddenly, an hour after I'd come to work. What did I want to do with this gift of time and freedom? I considered who I might want to tell about what had just happened... my husband? No, I thought, that had better wait until I had some idea about where I might be able to find a new job. It wouldn't have been such a big deal if he wasn't so worried about his own, given this economy and the fact that he hadn't been there that long. And had messed some things up already, in that short time. Well, if worse came to worst, we could always move back in with his sister. But thinking this completely undid the happiness I felt standing outside my building—even though it was cold and damp—instead of being stuck behind my desk in a corner of the tenth floor.

A movie, I thought. I used to love going to movies during the day. When I was single and lonely, it got me through hours I hadn't believed I could survive. Is that melodramatic of me to say? An exaggeration? Probably. Probably I would have been fine. Yet when I think about that time I feel a shadow around my heart, and it scares me to remember the way it scared me to feel it back then.

I went to the big downtown theater a few blocks away from the office and bought a ticket for the first show. I couldn't have cared less about the movie, but it would get me through the next hour and fifty-two minutes of my life. Right before I would have turned away from the cashier—a hungover-looking young man—I felt a spurt of inspiration and said, "Hey, I want to buy a ticket for the next person. I can do that, right?"

He narrowed his eyes as if I'd been speaking a foreign language. Then he shrugged. "I guess." He ran my card again. "But this is a crazy-early showtime. What if nobody else comes?"

I told him that was okay, it was the thought that counted. He promised to give the free ticket to the next person who tried to buy one for my movie, and to tell that person that another customer had taken care of it. I thanked him, bought a big box of Junior Mints, and settled myself into the dark plush of the theater, feeling good about myself even though I'd just spent twelve dollars I should have saved.

The kid was right—not a lot of demand for a movie that starts at 10:20 a.m. I had the whole theater to myself until the previews were almost over, when another figure crept into the cave. Age and gender I couldn't tell, but I was glad to see whoever it was, both because I wanted company for the movie and because I figured the person would have good feelings toward *me*, assuming the ticket-seller had kept his promise.

From his profile I saw now that it was a man, and from his posture I saw that he was probably not so young. He wore jeans and a windbreaker, sneakers, and a Red Sox cap. So, probably not a work day for him, either. He was going gray, he was overdue for a haircut, and even from a distance I could tell that his glasses sat crooked on his face. I felt him locate me in my upper row. For a moment I was afraid he'd approach to thank me, just when the movie was starting. But instead he only tipped the cap in my direction and sat down heavily in an aisle seat, much closer to the screen than I would ever have wanted to be.

The movie was pretty bad, but that's what you get for choosing one for some reason other than that it's a movie you want to see. I enjoyed eating my Junior Mints, even though I knew I'd feel sick later. The guy whose ticket I bought didn't appear to have brought in anything from the concession stand. Should I have treated him to refreshments, too? No, that would have been too much.

I started making my way down the stair mountain during the credits, because I wanted to get away before he could thank me. Isn't paying it forward supposed to be anonymous? Was I going to screw this up, too?

But I didn't move fast enough, and I ended up standing right next to him when the lights came on. He smiled and gestured at the screen and said, "That was nice of you. I would have bought my own, but it's a nice surprise, for somebody to do that."

This close, I could see he wasn't quite as old as I'd thought at first, maybe new to his forties, like me. "It wasn't really my idea," I said, because compliments—well, let's just say I'm not a fan. "Somebody did it for me this morning. This was my way of evening things up." *So I don't have to worry about it anymore*, I thought about adding but didn't.

His smile shrank a little as I spoke, but it was still a smile. "Okay," he said. "Well, I guess it's my lucky day."

Then I felt bad for making it awkward. "Did you like the movie?" I asked.

He shrugged. "To be honest, I didn't pay that much attention. I was just here for something to do." Then it seemed to occur to him that this might offend me. "Oh, should I not have said that? It doesn't mean I don't appreciate what you did."

"Same!" I smiled. "I mean, I was here for the same reason. But since you weren't paying attention, let me tell you: it was pretty bad."

We got to talking. He told me his name was Nathan Shiverdecker, and I laughed. "Really?" I said, and he said, "Well, I go by Nate," which made me laugh again. I told him I'd never heard the name *Shiverdecker* before, and he said, "Yeah, I get that a lot."

I told him my name was Kate, even though it isn't, because I liked the rhyme of it—Nate and Kate—and it turned out he did, too. We walked out of the theater together and made similar noises of surprise, because despite every forecast, the sun had come out. I was surprised too at how warm it felt, because the winter had been so cold and that's what I was used to. It was lunchtime and people were everywhere on the Common, walking or sitting on benches with sandwiches, turning their faces up to the suddenly bright sky. "Now I feel guilty for spending all that time in the dark," I said. "Wasting how nice it turned out to be."

"Still plenty of it left," Nate said. "Want to have lunch from a truck?"

Who was this guy who had time to go to a movie in the morning and then eat lunch with a stranger? Then again, who was *I*? It couldn't hurt, I figured. Plenty of people around.

I mean what else was I going to do?

We walked over to the Frog Pond. It was between seasons—ice skating was over, and they hadn't installed the carousel or opened the spray pool yet—and I had to describe these things to Nate, how charming it all usually was, when he asked me about that bean-shaped concrete bowl in the ground.

I only got a Diet Coke, to offset the Junior Mints, but Nate bought a huge pretzel. Chunks of salt fell down the front of his jacket as we talked and ate. He was from Maine, he said. He'd come to town with his wife, who was a patient at the hospital a few subway stops from where we sat. In the mornings he couldn't visit her because the doctors were making rounds. He didn't tell me what she was in for, and I didn't ask, even though I wanted to.

"What were *you* doing back there?" he asked, nodding at the theater behind us.

"I got fired," I said. "Well, let go. A bunch of us did. I don't mind, really—it's just that right then, when they told me, I didn't know what to do with myself."

His lips tightened in sympathy. I appreciated that he didn't try to console me or tell me everything would turn out all right. I hadn't said things would be fine with his wife, after all. Who knew what was going on there? Maybe she was at that hospital, a famous one with hotshot doctors, for some last-ditch hope at a miracle cure.

"Can you believe me and her have never been to Boston before?" Nate said, after allowing a moment of silence for my job. "Never, in all the years we lived up there. Three hours away. Talk about a waste."

This time I was the one who waited a few ticks before talking. "Do you like where you live?" I asked, and when he nodded I said, "Well, it's not a waste then, to spend time where you want to be."

He looked at me as if I'd said something profound, which I knew I hadn't. But hey, maybe that's in the eye of the beholder, and I really had!

"Kids?" I asked, and he shook his head.

"Us either," I told him, and then we had something in common you can't count on, in people our age.

I could tell we both felt the flash of affinity. "It's a good and a bad thing," he said quietly. "Good because nobody's losing a mother." Okay, I thought. So that's it. "But bad because…" He couldn't finish.

"I know." We both knew. You can't explain it to someone who doesn't get it, and you don't have to explain it to someone who does.

I enjoyed talking to him—Nate Shiverdecker—and I felt sorry I'd given him a fake name.

Then I thought, It doesn't really matter what our names are. All that matters is that we're sitting here together, on this day that's hard for both of us, feeling warm under a sun we'd been told not to count on. Enjoying the company and hoping for each other that things go as well as they can, even though neither of us is going to jinx it by saying so. Sometimes it's better that way. I could tell Nate understood this the same way I did.

His phone buzzed and he looked at it, then said he had to get going. "I like to be there when she's awake," he told me. It almost sounded like an apology. "She has this book of poems on the bed-table, and she likes me to read to her before the pain pills kick in. They make her feel better, she says. The poems—not the pills."

I wanted so much to ask what the book was! But it would have delayed him. Instead I said, "Of course, go," and made a shooing motion in the vague direction of the hospital. He smiled before he turned and started walking, then turned back again to thank me. I told him he was welcome, and then I thanked him, too.

I sat there on the bench till I couldn't see him anymore. Children were hopping and screeching on the playground, and I watched them for a while. I worried they'd think I was some kind of kidnapper or pervert, but then I realized that the point of being a child is you don't know what a kidnapper or a pervert is. Even though I knew it was dumb I waved at one of the kids before I left, and she waved back. You could have tried to tell me beforehand how good that would feel, but I wouldn't have believed you.

On the way home I stopped at the library. When was the last time I'd gone in there? Damned if I could remember. I asked the librarian if they had any poetry, and she kind of laughed—but not in a mean way—and told me where to look. Most of the poets' names I'd never heard of, but I knew Emily Dickinson's. I felt nervous opening that big book, because I never took a poetry class or learned how to understand it. But I decided to just start reading, standing there in front of the shelf.

"I felt my life with both my hands
      To see if it was there—"

Oh! I made a sound in the library.

I checked the book out and brought it home. It's dinnertime and Sam's late, but when he gets here, I'll have to tell him I lost my job. Will I come right out and say it? Or is it a better idea to mention the movie first, and Nate Shiverdecker, and the nice hour we had together talking and laughing a little before he left to return to his sick wife and, just to stretch out my time in the bonus sun, I walked the long way to the underground train that would shoot me through dark tunnels to the underground garage?

We need to have more fun, I'll say, and Sam will say, "Pam, what makes you think we deserve to have more fun?" Or maybe he'll tell me we can't afford to have fun. We can't afford *not* to, will be my answer, and then maybe we'll argue. Or maybe he'll sit down at the table and put his head in his hands and say, *You're right. I'm sorry. We'll figure something out.*

However it goes, it will be a better conversation than the one we would have had if the day went the way it was supposed to. If it weren't for Nate Shiverdecker, and the woman in the Civic who charged my coffee to her card. Who knows? Maybe it's not such a bad idea to treat strangers as if they're people you care about. Maybe not everything is as dumb as I thought it was, including me.

Cliché

It was at a classical guitar concert my husband brought me to that I felt it for the first time. The guitarist was a young woman from Serbia—well, she *looked* young, but the program seemed to say that she had given more than a thousand performances, over a period of thirty years. *Was* that what it said? I watched her play the first movement of the partita in A minor by Bach (not that I would have recognized the piece or even the chord, myself). It occurred to me that she was holding her instrument the way she might hold a large child: on her lap, at an angle, the child's head even with her own. So, not exactly a Pietà, but not too dissimilar from one, either, especially if you were to look only at the woman's face. I've lived long enough to know that sorrow and reverence can appear the same.

She did not strum or pluck the strings as much as she whispered to them with her fingers—or at least, that's what it looked like to me, and I assumed that I saw what everyone else in the audience, seated in those chilly church pews, did. She didn't just play the guitar, she had a relationship with it. I suppose that's why she was so good, and why this hall was packed with so many people.

The guitarist was very beautiful, with her long dark hair and in her black and white dress. She did not even look forty. She must have been a prodigy, a child, when she performed for the first time. Wasn't there a war on, back then, where she came from? Had she taken up the instrument in spite of this, or possibly because of it? Or had the war made no difference at all?

As the second movement began I bowed my head to consult the program again, and that was when I felt it, the swift surge of disequilibrium that seemed to shake my brain up and down, then sideways. An electric-feeling crackle that was not pain as much as it was pressure, though there was some pain, too. It lasted only a moment, and when it was over I found it hard to believe that no one else, including my husband, had noticed—that's how hard it had struck me.

The sanctuary was extremely still. No one seemed to be moving except the guitarist, and she moved only her head and hands. The crinkle in my brain, though brief, had left me afraid it would happen again, and I knew I could not sit there in that closed, still space, yet I also knew that for decorum's sake I must wait for another pause in the music before I could leave my seat in the pew and then the room. Agony they were, those minutes. Though I am sure that the sounds coming from the guitar were as smooth and as beautiful as they had been before my internal disruption, I do not think I heard them.

Finally, the break between movements. As I collected my scarf and coat and handbag, I whispered to my husband that I needed to move to the back of the church. He was startled but he said, "I'll come with you," because that is the kind of man I was married to. Quickly, I told him no—we'd sat up front specifically so that he, an amateur guitarist, could watch the Serbian woman's fingers as she played—and so he remained in the pew as I whispered further that I'd see him at intermission and then scurried out to the vestibule, where a few young people affiliated with the guitar society gathered to listen to the concert from beyond the sanctuary doors. I took my awkward place among them, indicating though it was not true that the heat in the room had been the trigger for my need to escape.

The guitarist began the partita's third movement, then stopped herself. "My instrument is being very temperamental this evening," she told the audience, smiling, and they responded with an understanding swell of sound as she interrupted her performance to retune the strings. "I cannot let it continue in this way," she added, before embarking afresh on the *Sarabande*, and I thought, See? Just like a child—when it acts up she gives it a talking-to, until it's ready to behave again.

Standing in the vestibule, I felt a few more minor waves of the big one that had sent me seeking the safety of the back. At the intermission, Jack joined me and said that because I didn't feel well, we should leave. I told him I'd be fine as long as I could keep watching and listening from the rear. "Are you sure?" he asked, and I could tell it was the right thing; he'd looked forward to this concert for so long, and I could see how much he was enjoying it. And it would only be after this break that the guitarist would play the classical guitar piece that was Jack's favorite, the name of which I always forgot, the one that had inspired him to take up the guitar himself.

Besides, it was only because I'd insisted on it that I was even at the concert at all. Jack had planned to go by himself, thinking I wouldn't be interested, but when he told me this I said, "Why wouldn't I be interested?" and he bought another ticket.

He was concerned about me, of course. His measure of worry made it possible for me to subtract from my own. When the concert was over I told him to go out with his friends from the guitar society for a drink, as they had planned; in normal circumstances I would have joined them, but as it was I said I'd call for a ride home and go to bed. I could tell that Jack was torn between wanting to have fun and being the kind of husband he thought he should be. It would be dishonest of me to say I was not disappointed when he chose the fun, but saying this would make me the kind of wife I didn't think I should be. It wasn't fair of me. Was it fair? True, my symptoms had vanished by concert's end. On the other hand, who knew if they'd return? In any event, I told Jack to go ahead, ordered a ride, turned the lamp off forty minutes later, and slept through the night without waking at Jack's arrival, his nightly routine in the bathroom, or his coming to bed.

RECENTLY I'D HAD A BIRTHDAY, my fifty-sixth. Was that the source of my distress? I use those words—distress, disequilibrium—even though they are not the precise ones to describe what I felt in the sanctuary that evening, and for some time afterward. "Dizziness" is not quite right either, though it might be closer than the others.

I was at a loss to explain what was happening to me. I did suspect it had something to do with the birthday and with not quite believing the age I was, along with maybe a little fantasy that if I tried hard enough, I could find a way to change it.

I asked a friend who, though she is not a doctor, knows some medical things. Because of her personality, she takes those things and runs with them, straight into opinion and advice. I should consult an ear, nose, and throat specialist, she told me. Probably I suffered from positional vertigo, and they'd be able to determine this by looking at my eyes to see if they jumped or twitched in certain telltale directions.

I went to a place called The Balance Center had the tests done, but it wasn't any of the disorders they could identify. For a couple of days after my appointment I didn't feel the symptoms—the free-falling in my head, the confusing internal heat—and I thought Great, I'm over it, whatever it was. But the reassurance didn't last long.

The concert was on a Saturday night. On Sunday morning Jack was even more solicitous than usual, and I knew he felt guilty for having abandoned me for his friends. Well, for choosing to go out with them. But to be fair, I *was* fine both on the way home and afterward, and I woke up the next morning feeling like my old self. He brought two cups of coffee to the bed and we sat there drinking and watching a Sunday news show together. Then he made pancakes. It was a very warm spring day, welcome after last night's chill, and in the afternoon he asked if I felt up to a hike. We took our favorite trail through a nearby forest. If not for my episode of the night before, I think he would have asked his friend Tamir to play tennis instead of going on a hike with me. But as it was, we had a nice time. I followed him for most of the way and he held back twigs and branches so they wouldn't hit my face, and toward the end, where the trail was wider, we walked side by side and talked about how pretty a day it was—so mild for March, almost like summer—and our children. We don't always agree, Jack and I, about what we should expect of them. They don't of course live with us anymore and we don't support them, and Jack thinks we should leave them alone. Let them decide when and how often we should see each other, or even be in touch by phone or text. We did a good job, he'd said to me more than once in trying to bring me over to his way of thinking. They're *supposed* to be off doing their own things, living their own lives. If they don't call, we should take that as a good sign.

 Well, so he needs to see it that way, I get that. But not me. I think Jack's a little too rigid and a little out of touch, I think he doesn't realize as much as I do that things aren't the same now as when we were Penny and Phillip's age. It was easier to be on your own back then, less chaos in the world to manage, or at least it seemed that way. My kids needing me—that feels like the way it should be.

After we finished our hike that Sunday and returned to the car, Jack said something so outrageous, and in such an offhanded tone, that I was sure I'd heard him wrong. "Maybe it would have been better if we'd never had children, you think?"

I laughed and said, "Yeah, right," but then I saw he was serious. I stared at him across the Pathfinder's roof. "What are you talking about?" Now I felt a slow smile coming on, not because I still thought he was joking but because I tend to smile at the most perverse times—when it's the exact opposite of what I should be doing. "What would possess you to say a thing like that to me?"

He shrugged, which is not at all a gesture I was accustomed to seeing in him. That, as much as the question he'd just asked, caused me to tell him I needed a minute, a little more fresh air, before we went home.

But the shrug hadn't meant what I was afraid it did, that he didn't care. He was sorry, I could see that. He gave a wave and apologized and mumbled something about a dream he'd had overnight, after being with his friends from the music society. To their surprise and pleasure, the Serbian guitarist had joined them at the bar. She'd made quick work of downing three cocktails (which the rest of them ended up paying for) and dropped charmingly mangled American curse words into her charmingly accented speech, which was more or less constant except for when one of the others managed to ask a question, or compliment her, when she paused for a sip.

"That sounds disappointing," I said to Jack. "So I guess what she was presenting to everyone at the concert, the image of a devoted mother almost, was just a persona. A mirage."

We'd started the drive back home from the forest, but when I said this Jack took his eyes away from the road to turn and look at me. "You thought she looked like a mother? That was the furthest thing from my mind."

"I just meant the way she was holding it, the guitar." Why did I feel the need to justify my impression? It was my impression, nothing more. I was making no claims about how things actually *were*—only about how they seemed to me.

Jack had returned his focus to the road. "Well, she's not a mother. Which was precisely my point."

"You said you had a dream?" I asked, not really wanting to understand what his point had been.

He nodded, still looking ahead. "It was one of those dreams where you're yourself, but in an entirely different life. Different house, different job, different... you know, not the same people around."

He'd been about to say different spouse or wife, of course. So, I didn't need to be told about the rest of the dream. Obviously, he'd been married in the dream to the Serbian guitarist; they did not have any children; and Jack was happier than he felt in real life, as my husband and as the father of two who were not children anymore but who (could this really be what he was saying?) might not have been worth it.

"I'm trying to figure out," I said, "if what you're telling me is that you never loved Phil and Penny."

"Of *course* I love Phil and Penny." The fact that my question seemed not to surprise him dismayed me even more. We'd arrived home, but we remained in the car to finish whatever this was. "But that's because we had them. *Have* them. They're real people, not abstractions. I was talking about what if we'd decided not to. We wouldn't miss what we'd never had."

"Well, I just can't go there," I told him, using an expression I happen to hate.

Jack said, "You shouldn't be so involved in their lives."

Was this a change of subject, or was it the same one? I couldn't tell. "But I don't mind. I *want* to be."

"That's not the point."

There were a lot of *points* he was trying to get across to me, it seemed. I left the car and went inside the house, and after a while Jack followed. At the sink I stood and filled a glass with cold, cold water, then drank it all in a series of gulps. He watched me do it, waited until I'd set the empty glass down, then asked, "How's your head, anyway? Any more of that dizziness?"

"It's not dizziness, exactly. It's more like—"

But I wasn't sure how to finish. He waited, until I smiled and shook my head and said, "Never mind." It was a relief to him, I saw, and a few minutes later he was on his way out to meet Tamir at the courts.

I opened my computer and searched for the Serbian guitarist's performances on video. Jack was wrong and I was right: the way she held that thing was *exactly* the way a mother holds a big child, one who won't be sitting in her lap for very much longer. Maybe one who is sitting there for the very last time. I considered bringing it up again when Jack returned, then decided not to. What would have been the point?

AT DINNER THAT NIGHT I SAID INSTEAD, "So what do you imagine your life would look like, without children? I mean, *our* life? Whatever it is, couldn't you still do it—couldn't *we*? You're the one who's always saying we should leave them alone now. That *I* should. If there's something you want to do now that we didn't have a chance to do when they were little, when they were living here, I'm all ears. I'm all in. We can have a fresh start, a second chance."

I was speaking in clichés, I realized. I don't like to resort to them, but sometimes you just have to, because they say the thing better than you could. And in this case it wasn't so bad, because I knew clichés were among the things my husband didn't mind.

But he was shaking his head, along with giving me that little smile I've learned to live with even though I have always hated it more than I hate clichés. *You're being silly*, the smile says. It *thinks* it's saying something else (or Jack does)—maybe *You're sweet*, or *I get a kick out of you*—but after all these years I've learned to interpret, to translate, and I know exactly what he is saying to me with that smile.

"Those are nice ideas," he told me. "But there's no such thing as a fresh start, at our age. Right? You know better. You know that as well as I do."

"No, I don't know it. I don't believe that." I would have liked to go on to say that I didn't appreciate his telling me what I did or didn't know, but I was afraid of bringing on the problem in my head again—the dizziness, the disorientation. I had done a little reading about it online after looking up the guitarist's videos, and more than one website cited stress as a possible source. So, I was trying to keep myself calm in case stress was my trigger, even though I had not felt at all stressed the night before while sitting in the sanctuary and listening to the beautiful woman play her beautiful music.

Or had I? I was not sure of anything now. "Do you want to take a vacation?" I asked Jack. "Do you want to downsize? Buy a new car?" More than one of my friends had a husband who, despite recognizing the cliché of it, bought a conspicuous car after he turned fifty. "Whatever it is, just tell me. I'm sure we can make it work."

Jack laughed, but there was no amusement in it. "You must not think very much of me," he said, "if you think my spiritual condition can be improved by a new car."

I was surprised to hear him use the word "spiritual." It wasn't one I'd ever associated with him before.

"Then what?" I'd made a pasta salad for supper, and the mayonnaise was melting in the heat. I got up to put it back in the fridge. While I was setting it on the shelf Jack said, behind me, "I'm going to marry Milena."

Later, I'd realize that he waited to say it until my back was literally turned. I heard him, but before closing the fridge I adjusted a few things to make more room. Then I shut the door and asked, as if it were the most pertinent piece of information I needed just then, "Who's Milena?"

But of course, I knew. He was talking about the dark-haired, mother-mimicking, cocktail-swilling, curse-uttering, guitar-cradling Serb.

Tears followed, not all of them mine. Shouted sentences, whispered ones. They'd known each other for seven months, he told me; she'd taught the classical guitar workshop Jack had gone to, in Boston, the one I gave him for his birthday after I asked what he would consider a special gift. Penny had come to spend that Saturday night with me. I hadn't told her I invited her because I was afraid to be alone in our house at night; I just said I thought it might be a nice time for a mother-daughter sleepover. We actually did have a nice time, though I had to listen to a lot of complaining. It had been all I could do not to utter those fatal words "When I was your age," and I do think I could have offered her some useful advice from my experience both when I was her age and since, but it would have backfired. She might even have gotten so mad as to abandon me before the "sleepover" part of our plan, which had been, after all, the point.

I think she appreciates me as much as any twenty-five-year-old appreciates her parents. Her brother, who's a year older, the same. They want us when they want us, and they don't want us when they don't. That's the way it should be, as Jack's always telling me.

But what would Phil and Penny think when they found out about their father carrying on with the Serbian guitarist? Not only "carrying on," but wanting to trade in our marriage for a marriage to her?

And what did it mean about me that this—how the kids would react—was the first thing I wondered, after Jack said he was going to marry Milena? In other words: what did *I* think about it? What was *my* reaction?

I went back to the table and sat across from him. There was a fleck of black olive on his placemat and ordinarily this would have bothered me, ordinarily I would have popped up again to remove it, but at a moment like this, who cared? Still, my eyes stayed on the black bit, and pretty soon Jack was staring at it, too.

"I can't tell you how sorry I am about all this," he said. "I didn't go looking for it, if that makes any difference. I didn't try to make it happen. But since it has, I can't pretend it didn't. Or ignore it. That wouldn't be good for me, and—really, I mean this—it wouldn't be good for you, either."

Don't tell me what's good for me! I heard the words as if I'd screamed them, but I hadn't even murmured them aloud. After a few minutes I asked, "Can you just tell me why? I mean, I get that she's young. *Younger.* And beautiful. But you're not a shallow person. A shallow man. How could it be only those things?" In my pocket, I remembered, I had a tissue. I pulled it out, picked up the speck of olive, and squeezed it inside my fingers. Then I squeezed the tissue inside my fist.

"No, no, no. It isn't those things at all." He forced himself to look directly at me, or at least that was my impression—that he had to force himself to do it. He did not follow up by telling me what things it *was*.

Recuerdos de la Alhambra—that's the title of his favorite song. It popped into my head at that moment. I dare you to listen to that piece, played by someone who knows what they're doing, without feeling more than you bargained for. It was playing in my head, now.

"I wish you would yell at me," Jack said. "Get mad. I'm mad at *myself*, for letting this happen. Where's your anger?"

He said it the way he might say *Where are your car keys?* But he knows me better than that. I wasn't going to show any anger, and it didn't have anything to do with not feeling upset.

"*This* feels like a dream, to me," I told him. I heard the tone of my voice, pathetic, and hated myself for it. I stood up too suddenly and had to grab the back of my chair to keep from toppling. Jack was at my side immediately, helping me back into the seat.

"More dizziness?" he asked, and he brought me some water.

"Maybe I have a brain tumor," I said. Why on earth would I have smiled when I said this? But I did, even as Jack winced.

He didn't actually move out, join Milena on her tour, until the doctors determined that I didn't in fact have a tumor. During this time of fracturing to our family, I had to be very careful about how I moved my head. No sudden turns to the side, no looking down at too sharp an angle. And absolutely no lying flat on my back. Despite my vigilance, it still happened sometimes, during those weeks before Jack left—the crinkle in my vision, the slight bolt of pain in my forehead, that signaled the incipience of what I'd come to think of as a "spell." At some point during that period I'd been looking at some old family photos, and remembered that my grandmother had suffered similar episodes, and that she called them *spells*.

What had she done about them? Lain down. With a wet cloth across her forehead. I refused to do this—not because I scorned my grandmother's solution for herself, but because I was afraid if I lay down other than when I was supposed to, I'd never get back up.

Phil and Penny were confused at first—disbelieving—then furious, when their father left. It should've touched me, how hurt and angry they were on my behalf even more than their own, but instead it made me feel sorry for Jack. Yes, he'd asked me after our hike that Sunday if I agreed with him that we'd have been better off without kids, but in the meantime I'd figured out that the question was just his defense against feeling the pain he was about to cause our children. I knew how much he loved them. For that matter, I knew he loved me, too; it wasn't anything I'd done, or failed to be, that sent him into the supple arms of the Serbian guitarist.

The kids came around a lot more, once I was living alone. Penny offered herself up for routine sleepovers. Over wine one of those Saturday nights, she asked out of the blue if I knew anything about gorillas. I wanted to say, "Why would I know anything about gorillas?" but I held it back. She'd been reading a book about Dian Fossey's research, and I knew my only role was to appear interested, ask questions, and let her say what she knew.

"The dominant gorillas aren't the biggest and most physically powerful," she told me, "the way it is with humans. The alpha males are the most nurturing with the babies, whether they're the father or not." She went on to quote Fossey as saying that the more you learn about how dignified gorillas are, the less you want to hang out around people.

I refrained from asking why Penny was telling me this. Was there a point to it in our own lives? Jack wasn't very tall or very loud in the human world. You wouldn't call him an alpha. So maybe what my daughter was saying was that we shouldn't have expected as much of her father as we did. Or was she saying we should expect more? I wasn't sure.

Neither of the kids spoke about their father directly, and I couldn't tell if they thought they were sparing me or themselves by largely omitting any mention of him from our conversations. Jack called every week or so, to make sure I was doing okay and to answer the questions I had about things he'd always taken care of that now fell to me.

I asked how he was too, of course. The first calls came from Germany, Ireland, and Spain. Then, after four or five months, the two of them were "recharging" at Milena's country house outside Belgrade. It sounded idyllic; they could see mountains from their bedroom, he told me, and ride their bikes to the beach.

It was tacky of him to mention their bedroom, but I forgave him because I could tell right away he regretted it. He's never been the most tactful person, or the best at reading a room.

When he asked how my dizziness was, how often it was happening, he sounded almost disappointed when I told him it had stopped. Was that possible—for him to feel disappointed by this news? I didn't trust my interpretation. Or I did, but it made me feel bad, so I told myself I was hearing something that wasn't there.

I made plans with my friends more—much more—than I had when I wasn't single, which is how I thought of myself now, single, even though there had been no legal change yet to my status as Jack's wife. I kept waiting for him to say something about it during one of our calls, or for an envelope to arrive from a lawyer containing divorce papers, but neither happened. I began walking every morning with a group of birdwatchers, and learned how to make paella and re-grout the tub. I installed an alarm system in the house so I could sleep easier. I got my hair cut and bought some new clothes because the old ones didn't fit anymore. I don't think it was only because I lost weight; I was carrying myself in a different way. At least, that's what Penny told me. I looked good, she said. She said she was proud of me. Well, that was a flip in the script from when I always said I was proud of *her*. She never had much confidence as a kid, and I did my best to boost it. It paid off—now look at her, only three years out of college and she's something called a media operations analyst. It's not what she likes doing, not even close, but I keep telling her if she pays her dues, eventually she'll get what she wants. I tell her this because it's what I need to believe. What could be worse than watching the death of your own child's dreams?

In November, I received an email from the guitar society informing me that Milena Petrovic would be returning to reprise her concert of the year before, "by popular demand." I was surprised; Jack hadn't mentioned this in our most recent call. On an impulse, I bought a ticket and on the night of the event I drove myself into the city—something I used to avoid—and got to the church early enough to take a seat near the front, so I could watch the guitarist's fingers as Jack had wanted to the year before. Of course I'd had no idea at the time how intimately he knew those fingers. But aside from that, I understood it would help me appreciate the music, to watch it being made from a close range.

As for my seat near the front, I had no fear of becoming dizzy, as I had the last time I'd sat in this space. For nearly six months now I'd felt completely solid in my footing and in my mind, with no disturbances to either my physical or psychic stability. I would not need to leave the sanctuary and retreat to the vestibule, I knew. I'd be able to bend my head to look at the program all I wanted—the bad feelings were not going to come back.

I figured I'd see Jack there, but he was obviously surprised to see me. His whole body reacted, not just his face, when I caught his eye across the aisle and lifted my hand in a greeting. There was still time before the concert began, so he came over to take an awkward perch on the pew next to me, after leaning over to kiss the cheek I offered.

Had he planned on calling to tell me—and the children—he was in town? Of course, he told me. They'd only flown in from Vienna the night before. What had he been doing all day? "Well, distracting Milena, mostly. Or trying to," he said. "I don't think I help things much, actually. She gets so nervous before every performance." I tried to identify what it was I heard in his voice then: confession? Apology, and if so, to whom? More, it sounded to me as if he wanted me to feel sorry for him, which I could not do.

"I would have called you tomorrow," he went on, maybe seeing this in my face. "In fact I would have called before we got here, but…" He stopped himself, probably understanding that I'd already guessed he and Milena were having troubles. "But now I don't have to," he said, brightening to give me the smile he knew was my favorite. "Are the kids around? Maybe we could all have dinner together. I mean I haven't asked Milena, but she has tomorrow night off."

I shrugged. "Well, I'm free. That would be fine with me." Would it? I wasn't so sure, but I felt the need to give the answer I did. "I don't know about Phil and Penny—they might be around and they might not. I haven't spoken to either of them in a while."

The lights dimmed, and Jack hurried back to his seat. Why, though? He could have remained next to me.

We did end up getting together for dinner the following night, although I'm guessing it goes without saying that Milena didn't join us to make it five. I proposed meeting at a restaurant, but Jack said why didn't we keep it simple, and just have a barbecue at home.

When he arrived alone I asked, "She's not coming?"

Phillip looked at me as if he hadn't heard right. "What? You invited *her*?"

"I was trying to be civil," I told him. "Civilized." I couldn't tell if Jack was listening to us or not; he was checking the grill.

"There's civil and then there's… well, I don't know what the right word would be," Phillip muttered. "But I wouldn't stay two minutes if she was here."

"It's better this way," Penny said.

I hadn't yet learned to barbecue, and during the months Jack lived in Europe, the grill had sat on the patio without being used. It wouldn't catch when he tried to ignite it, so I carried the plate of patties back into the house and cooked them on the stove. This turned out to be a good thing, because it started to rain. Phillip and Penny were cold to their father at first, but then they warmed up. There were hugs. There was laughter. At some point after we'd eaten

Jack said, "Should we take a photo? To mark the occasion?" No one asked *What occasion*, but the four of us lined up in a row and Phillip, the tallest, held his phone high above us all.

"For God's sake smile, Dad," he said. Next to me I could feel the stretch and strain of Jack trying, but being told how to pose has never sat well with him. I also understood that when he'd suggested a photo he thought I'd get out my old Canon with its tripod and timer; he hates the concept of selfies, not to mention the word itself. It's not my favorite either, but you have to choose your battles. And sometimes the moment's lost if you don't capture it right away.

Whoever said the camera never lies, though—that person had it wrong. Jack's the one who looks apprehensive, as if he's not sure I'll take him back when he asks. But I know better. Of course he's sure. I, on the other hand, appear downright giddy at the sight of my husband back home, flipping meat on the grill as if he had never left.

But look closer and you'll see I hold my head steady, because I can tell it's about to start spinning. I'm bracing against what I know, now, comes next. His question, my answer. Tears and smiles, not all of them mine. Doesn't it mean something—won't it be *some* kind of victory—if I don't let myself get blindsided the way I did the first time?

Tribute

to Larissa Lee and Bill Knott

I came into the house complaining about our mail carrier, who'd left the mailbox door open again.

"So leave him a note." Coco didn't look up from the page she was reading. "Leave *him* some mail, for a change. Maybe that's what he's waiting for."

"Ha," I said, to humor her. "No, but I'm serious. How lazy do you have to be?"

She shrugged; she was immersed in the biography of some woman I'd never heard of. Two of the four envelopes I tossed. The third was from my aunt in a memory-care unit in Florida, who sent me birthday cards about once a month. Sometimes I opened them but more often I didn't, because I felt sad and angry that she was so out of it, and I worried the same thing would happen to me someday.

The fourth envelope I slit open with my finger. If it had been addressed to Coco, who couldn't stand ragged edges, she'd have used a proper letter opener. But I'd never had that kind of patience, especially when I felt annoyed, as I did now about the mailbox and my aunt not being able to get things right.

"Dear Audrey,

You are receiving this because I have been privileged to treat you at The Ravell Cancer Institute. It is my great sadness to inform you that I am suspending my practice after my own diagnosis of advanced cancer. Your health management will be transferred to one of the excellent clinicians on our staff. I am aware that this will be hard news to hear, and I am truly sorry for the emotional disruption it may cause. Please do not allow it to interfere with your recovery and well-being, and know that it has been my honor to provide you care. I will continue to wish you all the best.

>Yours with hope,
>Lucia Dove, M.D."

"Oh, my God." I dropped the page on the table, then picked it up again to make sure I understood what I'd just read. I waited for Coco to say "What?" or to look up, and when she didn't I said again, louder, "Oh, my *God.*"

Now she did look over, with her thumb stuck in the page to mark her place. She only raised her eyebrows, but I didn't know whether she was asking why I'd exclaimed or showing me she wished I hadn't interrupted her reading.

"It's from Dr. Dove."

Hearing this she set the book aside, got up, came to me with an apprehensive air, and held her hand out for the piece of paper.

"It's not about me," I hastened to tell her, touched by the fear I saw in her face. "*She* has cancer. This is a letter to all of her patients, saying she's suspending her practice."

"Suspending," Coco said, letting out a long breath. "So maybe she thinks she can be treated and then come back."

"But it doesn't say anything like that. About resuming." I took the page and studied it again. "Also—" I pointed at the words—"*advanced cancer.*"

She nodded. I knew and appreciated that she would not try further to turn this letter into something other than what it was. "I like that it's addressed to 'Audrey,'" she said, "instead of 'Dear Patient' or 'Ms. Carnell.' And to sign it '*with hope*'—" She put a hand over her heart.

"I know. That's just like her." I thought about the gentle smile the doctor had always given me before she left the poison room. I'd had a crush on her—a patient-crush, the kind anyone would feel for the person who saved their life—but I'd never mentioned this to Coco. Probably I would have if the doctor had been ugly. I know how that sounds, but I can't help it, it's true. Coco met her at my initial radiation consult, and afterward we'd agreed that Amy Adams should play her in the movie because of the red hair, though Dr. Dove (we also agreed) was even nicer to look at than the actress. She was a real person right in front of us, after all. No makeup or filters. You could tell she was good at her job and you could tell she cared—she didn't have to act at either of these things.

And her name was so perfect for her: Lucia Dove. Light and peace. She even kind of cooed when she spoke, though in a soothing rather than sappy way.

"So this means she's dying, I guess." I usually had to say hard things out loud before they sank in. "But she has a kid, a little one. Like, still believes in the tooth fairy." I closed my eyes to see the memory more clearly. "She showed me a picture of him with his teeth missing. How many doctors do that?"

Coco nodded again. She already knew all this. "She's only in her thirties," I went on. "Ten years younger than me. It's not fair."

For this is what I'd been feeling since the gist of the letter became clear to me. The person who'd cured me was now terminal herself? Not fair and not possible. Yet here we are.

Coco, also musing aloud: "Do we think it's just coincidence that someone who spends five days a week in a basement filled with radiation ends up with cancer at a young age?"

"Yes. Or at least, *I* do." I wasn't generally a bigger believer in coincidence than Coco was, but if Dr. Dove had gotten cancer radiating her patients, then I myself was complicit, and this simply would not do. "They always went into a little side room after the steel doors shut. They called it the bunker. Where they sent the radiation from."

I remember how alone I always felt, watching the bunker door close, sealing me in by myself to lie and look up at the ceiling where a video screen showed revolving beach scenes. If I turned my head, I could see people through the window separating the toxic room from the safe one—Dr. Dove and whatever resident she was supervising, along with a technician or two. Though I understood that they were probably discussing their plans for the weekend or where to go for lunch, and that I was just one of dozens of patients they'd implant with seeds and radiate that day, it made me feel better to imagine they were talking about me.

In the moments after the beams were shut off but before Dr. Dove and her assistant returned to set me free, I sometimes folded my hands on my chest above the hospital gown, a gesture of self-consolation. *It's okay, body*, I might have been telling it. *I know I haven't always taken the best care of you. But that'll change now, after what you've been through.* Once I'd been released and put my clothes back on, then managed to navigate the narrow and nerve-racking hospital parking garage, I drove home, stopping on the way for a chocolate-and-vanilla-swirl soft-serve cone, always the same treat. It was not what Coco would have considered taking the best care of myself, but I knew better than she did about this.

A poet had lived in our neighborhood. We didn't know him, and we hadn't realized he was a poet until after he died; we used to see him walking fast along the street, his lanky old body following the lead of his head with its flyaway white hair, and say to each other, "There goes Albert Einstein again." He didn't really look like Albert Einstein, but it was clear he possessed both intention and seriousness, and though Coco and I joked, I knew we both wished we had destinations we were as excited about as he seemed to be.

After he died, we read one of his poems in a tribute written by a former student.

> "Going to sleep, I cross my hands on my chest.
> They will place my hands like this.
> It will look as though I am flying into myself."

It reminded me of the way I'd subconsciously (I saw then) blessed myself, each time I'd finished with a treatment and was about to get up from the table in the radiation room. When I woke in the nights during that time, this is how I lay in trying to get back to sleep, always with the words *flying into myself* chanting across the dark velvet of my mind.

"It's just a coincidence," I insisted to Coco, about the news that my oncologist was herself dying of cancer. Then I groaned and this time she did ask, "What?"

"I can't believe I let myself get so upset over the mailbox door being open. Ten minutes ago I was filled with rage, and about what? It couldn't *be* more trivial."

"You had no idea what was about to happen. What you were about to find out." She gestured toward the page I'd placed on the table carefully, as if it were valuable. Well, it *was*. "Don't be so hard on yourself."

"But it's ridiculous. Remember the resolutions I made, after my surgery? I wasn't going to waste time on stupid things anymore. I was going to quit my job and find a more meaningful one. Volunteer. Meditate. Exercise. Really listen to other people, and not do so much talking myself." I remembered lying on the couch with my hands arranged in the flying-into-myself position, feeling so overwhelmed by the poignancy of a second chance that my chest pulsed with it and hot tears streamed down my cheeks.

At the time it had felt essential to change my life. Where had it all gone—that conviction? I still felt grateful, still felt lucky that my own disease had been caught in time to be removed and radiated away. Yet here I was complaining about the mailbox door.

Coco came over and wrapped her arms around me from behind. "Having cancer doesn't turn you into a saint," she said. "You're never going to be immune to the stupid things."

But she could not persuade me. Dr. Dove's letter had hit home, hard, and I vowed not to forget the crucial message I'd received now for the second time.

BUT, OF COURSE, I DID FORGET IT. It was easier to imagine what might be happening in the doctor's closing-down life than to figure out how to open my own. During the time I'd set aside to research possible volunteer "opportunities," as I learned they were called (where could I do the most good—with elderly people, or children? And was I allowed to consider which I'd prefer? I suspected not), I Googled Lucia Dove instead. It turned out she was married to a veterinarian; she lived in the town next to my own; and she routinely raised money for charitable organizations by running 10Ks.

I was not a runner myself, but that didn't mean I couldn't become one. I found an app that would ease me in slowly, walking first and then building up to whatever distance I programmed it for. I set my target as 10K and registered for an event at the end of the summer.

I could have chosen to practice on the track at the high school, but instead I created a route that would take me through the neighborhood where Lucia Dove lived. I wore sunglasses and my hair tucked under a hat, even though I doubted she'd recognize me if she looked out the window at a jogger plodding down her street. Still, if any doctor might notice and identify her patient in such a circumstance, she'd be the one.

The first few days, I saw no activity in her house or yard when I passed, and I didn't know whether to feel deflated or glad. What did I hope to see? Her husband, her son? The doctor herself?

This was it, I realized—I wanted to see what it looked like, my doctor dying. Why? In case I ever had to do it myself? Because I was one of those people who kept pressing my tongue into the gap where the tooth used to be, to see if it still hurt? Because I needed to remind myself that it was her and not me?

Only once in the first two weeks of my "training" did I see anyone outside the house, a boy of five or six on the trampoline in the backyard. I almost missed him because he wasn't bouncing or even standing, but lying with his head against the mesh enclosure, a tablet propped on his stomach as he swiped a finger across the screen.

Had he been told his mother was dying? If so, was he searching on the tablet for something to help him understand this, or to forget it? I guessed forget. And in the next moment I knew I was right, when the sound of video-game music blasted across the yard and the boy began poking furiously, punctuating his efforts with exclamations I could hear from where I stood watching. *No no no you don't!* and then, maybe to an invisible friend who sat beside him, a sigh accompanying the report: *I losed*. I forced myself to start running again, but had to stop a few steps later because of a stitch in my side.

BEFORE THEN COCO KNEW I WAS WORKING UP to run a 10K, but I hadn't told her the part about taking a route past Dr. Dove's house. I hadn't told her because she would have considered it stalking, which it was.

But that night, after seeing the boy on the trampoline, I confessed, because I wanted—I *needed*—to talk about what it made me feel. "Don't you think she must wonder if he'll remember her?" I asked. "Don't you think she figures her husband will get married again, and the kid'll have a stepmother, and he'll only know his real mother from photos and the things his father tells him? How do you think she can stand that? I mean, would *you* be able to? Do you think she wakes up in the middle of the night and—"

"Audrey. Stop." Coco shook her head and did her best to smile, even though I could tell she didn't really feel it. "You're doing it again."

"Doing what?"

"Obsessing. Perseverating. Whatever you want to call it." She sat back as if I'd exhausted her, which I probably had. "I get why. But it's not doing you any good. And anyway, you're talking about how *you* would feel. Right? In that situation. You don't know anything about what *she's* actually feeling."

"But how could she not feel those things?"

Coco shrugged. "For all you know, she's found some way to focus on the good stuff in the time she has left."

I doubted this, but I knew better than to argue, and I resolved not to bring up my dying doctor at the dinner table, at least for a while.

And for a few days, I made myself run at the track instead of the route by the doctor's house. But then it got the better of me—the obsession, the perseveration—and I headed to her street again. I imagined I might see her sitting on the front stoop with her arms wrapped around her knees in an embrace of herself, maybe even rocking from the pain of what she was forced to endure. She'd either be resting her head on her knees, too weary to hold it upright, or staring straight ahead at something the rest of us couldn't see. In either case, in all my fantasies, the red hair would be covering her face, meaning she wouldn't notice me. And I wouldn't have to witness what it looked like to feel death coming.

The house seemed quiet as it usually did, and I figured it would be another day without a sighting. Then I heard sounds in the backyard, and sensed movement without understanding what it was.

Did I dare move closer? A fence separated the driveway from the yard, and I could mostly hide behind it if I wanted a better look. But was it wrong of me to do this? And what made me hesitate more, even though I know I should be ashamed to admit it: What if I got caught?

But they weren't real questions. I knew I wasn't going to resist. I crept forward to see that the rhythmic sound came from someone bouncing on the trampoline. The boy I'd seen the other day?

No: it was the doctor herself! I gasped at the sight, though it sounded more like a laugh.

She wore a T-shirt and cutoffs. Bare feet and no bra. I was shocked to see she'd gotten a buzz cut… but no, of course she hadn't—the hair was only trying to grow back in. It wasn't red as it had been, just an ordinary and undistinctive brown. She didn't look like an actress anymore. But you wouldn't have guessed she was a very sick person, either.

Then I took a cautious step closer and thought, Oh, maybe you *would* guess. She couldn't jump very high, and her balance was off, to the point that I winced watching, worried she would fall. A sound came from her, too, which I couldn't identify. A laugh like my own? This was what I wished, but then I realized it was the noise of her breathing, the extra effort she had to make to keep up with her own speed. A chuffing exhalation, then a thin high whistle when she took air in.

I was tempted to think it was sad. It *looked* sad—here she was the opposite of how I remembered her, when she'd been so sure-footed and sure-handed and… well, beautiful. All that hair and good health.

But it wasn't really as sad as I'm making it out to be. She was trying! She'd land with her knees bent, then take off again using her arms as propellers the way kids do. You wouldn't have called it soaring, but she wasn't a total flop at it either.

As I watched her, mesmerized, she came to an abrupt, unsteady landing and glanced over to where I stood. Then she waved. Wait—was that what she was doing? I felt a momentary thrill, even as I panicked at thinking she'd seen me. I held back another gasp, pulling the bill of my cap down over my forehead and taking a few steps back.

From my new position, I could see through a window of her house into the kitchen, where a man and a boy looked out at *her*. It was the boy from the other day, who'd been jabbing at the tablet as he lay on the trampoline. These two, her husband and son, were the ones she'd waved at, I realized. Relief that she hadn't seen me twisted with disappointment in my gut.

The boy waved back and turned to say something to his father; I could almost hear him crying *Look!* The father smiled as the boy scrambled down from the window, disappeared for a second or two, then burst out the back door in a streak toward the trampoline. He pitched himself inside the net, and his mother grabbed up both his hands with her own. They began jumping together, turning every which way, falling on their knees and lifting each other back up again. Arms and legs tangled, both laughing and shrieking like there was no tomorrow. Well, there wasn't!

She was flying into herself, I understood that. But she was flying into him, too.

Through the window, I watched the husband brace himself against the counter and bow his head.

I ran. My legs carried me faster than they ever had, even though I made no effort at all. A strange lightness moved through my limbs, as if I were suddenly buoyant, airborne, myself. All these years later I remember that run the way you remember other miracles in your life, marveling that they could ever have happened and wondering what made you so lucky.

If you'd asked me back then I would have said that of course I'd go first, because Coco was younger and in better shape and ate all the right things, but instead here we are. A lot has left me by now, but more remains, including the memory of the day my life really did change, the day I began seeing the world in a different way from the way I'd seen it before. When I got home from that run I found the mailbox door open, only instead it looked like a dog's mouth with the tongue hanging down. It didn't annoy me, it was adorable! Among the bills and solicitations sat an envelope from my aunt. When I saw it I felt happy because I loved my aunt, and I knew she loved me back and wanted nothing but good things for me and, for that matter, everyone else in the world. I carried the mail into the house, where Coco was eating a peach and reading the book about the woman I'd never heard of. "Guess what," I said, waving the card, "it's my birthday again," and she looked up at me and smiled.

Attached

It was me who said we'd regret it if one of us didn't stay home with the baby, at least for the first year. We both understood that by "one of us" I meant me. My job was the more replaceable, and less rewarding than Harold's in every sense of the word. I pretended to be at least a little sorry about having to give it up, but the truth was that it had gotten old by then and I couldn't wait to leave, especially for as good a reason as starting a family.

At first, I was over the moon about my new life. Healthy son, open schedule, time to myself during his naps. I thought I'd spend that time reading, and at the beginning I tried, but I always found myself dozing over the book, so instead I took to lying on the couch and napping myself with the TV on low in the background. If Harold called, I muted the volume. Why? I told myself it was so I'd be able to hear him better. But the truth was that I didn't want him to know I had the TV on. I was embarrassed. I didn't want him to think I was slacking off being a mother, even when Hal was asleep.

Maybe I shouldn't admit this, but I didn't want to name the baby after my husband. I saw what that did to my brother, but even if I hadn't, it seemed like asking for trouble. I wanted my baby to have a name of his own, a fresh one picked just for him. But Harold had a strong feeling in the other direction, and I gave in.

The baby had a lot of energy in the mornings. That's when he laughed the most and played the hardest. He was active when he woke up in the afternoons, too, but I'd call it more alert—a mental energy—than moving-around liveliness.

He was smart, it was obvious. Thoughtful, even. I'm not just saying that because I'm his mother. You would have seen it yourself. After our stop in the mailroom every day, I wheeled him in his stroller to the yard outside our building, and I'd sit there with a magazine open on my lap but I wasn't really reading—I was watching Hal and listening to him. He'd catch my eyes and communicate something, whatever was going on in his little brain right then, and he'd send me a smile that told me he understood we were connected, now and forever, and he was as happy about this as I was.

That smile went right to my gut. It moved something in there. It was the strongest thing I'd ever felt in my life. Almost *too* strong—almost scary.

I asked Harold if he knew what I was talking about. How he felt when Hal smiled at him. He just said, "Good! Really good," so I knew it was different for the two of them. Not worse, just different.

One day when Hal and I were out in the yard and he looked at me as if he wished he knew words, I remembered reading a novel that introduced the main character as an infant. The book described what was going on in the baby's mind. He understood what to do to get the grown-ups' attention—coo, make faces, cry with delight—but he also felt secretly amused by the way the adults made fools of themselves, prancing around and using silly voices to speak to him. He looked up with scorn from his crib at the giant clowns who assumed they understood more than he did, when he knew they did not.

Remembering this, I found myself tuning into my own baby's thoughts as we sat there and looked at each other. *You will always be the first person I ever loved*, I sensed him telling me. *Don't forget these times of you and me sitting here, not needing anything else. Do you have any idea how important you are?* A few lines connected to other people or things—*I love when Daddy makes those fart noises, don't you?* or *I like the sun on my face but not in my eyes*—but mostly what I allowed myself to "hear" had to do with his feelings about me, and about the two of us as a little team.

For his first birthday we had a bunch of people over, and Hal handled it pretty well. He didn't seem to mind being on display and the center of all that attention. I mean he cried a little when people sang *Happy Birthday*, but that was because his rowdy cousin Brianna shrieked the words instead of singing them, then clapped too loud right in the baby's face. *Get away from me, bitch!* I heard him thinking, and I had to hold back a laugh.

I figured he'd stop crying once the noise settled down and Brianna had been lured away by one of her uncles trying to tie a balloon in the shape of an elephant. But the balloon popped, Brianna began crying herself, and Hal jumped in my arms at the sudden shock of the sound. Poor kid, I thought, he has my nervous system. He started wailing all over again, and I went into his bedroom to find his pacifier.

The mere sight of it calmed him down; he reached for it and popped it into his mouth, and within a minute he was sucking away as if it held a flavor he couldn't get enough of. *Thank you. I love this thing.* Tears were still wet on his face, but the crying had stopped. From across the room, Harold gave me a thumbs-up. There was more of his family at the party than mine, and even though he would have sided with me officially, I knew it mattered to him, what they thought of Hal and what kind of parents they took us to be.

"You really should be weaning him off the binky by now," Harold's sister said. "You don't want his teeth coming in funny."

"He doesn't have any teeth yet," I told her.

"Plus," she went on, as if I hadn't said anything, "he should be learning to soothe himself. Bri gave hers up by eight months."

I saw no point in letting her know that if she really wanted me to take her advice about anything involving child behavior, she wouldn't use Brianna as an example. I just smiled and carried Hal into his bedroom for a change he didn't need. *Good call. That kid is crazy! Let's kill some time in here.* We played a little and I read him a book, so by the time I brought him out again we were both back in a party mood.

It wasn't that night but the next that Harold said, "So should we be thinking about the binky? Getting rid of it, I mean?"

"Oh, no, not yet." I tried to hide how much the idea rattled me. Not only because I'd be losing a reliable method of calming Hal down, but because I knew how much pleasure and comfort it gave him to plop it in and start sucking. "You're not bringing this up because your sister said something, are you? Because you know that doesn't matter to me, right?"

This wasn't true, but I kept hoping that if I said it enough, it would be.

Harold shook his head. "That's not it. Or not that *mostly*. It just makes sense to me that it's better not to let him get too used to putting something in his mouth to make him feel better. Doesn't that make sense to you?"

Well, I saw his point, but I also didn't think there'd be any harm in giving our son a little more time with something so familiar, which he enjoyed so much. It would be a major disruption in his life when we took it away, and I hated to think of inflicting that on him. I promised to bring it up at Hal's next doctor's appointment, which would be his eighteen-month checkup. Harold agreed, even though I could tell he wasn't terrifically happy about waiting that long.

He deferred to me because the baby's development was my department. Things like sports, when it came time for that, and the college fund—those were his. We'd never said any of this in so many words, but it's the way things shook out, as Harold would have put it. The longer I stayed home instead of working, the more surprised I felt that we started divvying up tasks the same way our parents had. It would all change when I got my next job, I told myself. That wouldn't be long, right? When Hal turned two, I'd start looking. In the meantime, I told myself to take Harold's advice and enjoy being a full-time mom.

At the wellness checkup, the pediatrician said it was a good idea to "ditch the dummy." I kind of hoped Harold would forget about it, but after I gave the checkup report, he asked. The next day, during the time I'd set aside to read the story collection I'd picked up at the library, I scrolled through mommy blogs instead. I planned to tell Harold at dinner about my two favorites of the weaning suggestions I found there—the paci fairy, and the book we could read to Hal that would make him feel like a big boy—but before I could, Harold said he'd asked Drew at work how his baby had kicked the binky, and then he described how Drew and his wife had done it, pronounced their method brilliant, and said he wanted "us" to do it the same way.

"Okay," I said, but I kind of swallowed the word. What happened to the baby's development being my department? But Harold, not me, was the one who sat around all day talking strategies. "Should we try this weekend?"

"Oh. Okay." His smile folded, and I could tell it was in response to the *we*. On Friday night, as a kind of test, I hid the binky when we put Hal to bed, to see how fast he'd notice. He hadn't been in the crib twenty seconds when he began to fuss and pat the sheet around him, searching.

"Here you go, buddy," Harold said, producing the thing and receiving a crow of pure joy and gratitude in return.

"Well, that wasn't much of a test," I said. "You didn't even give it a chance."

He shrugged. "Let's give him one last weekend. Maybe it won't be such a big deal if we do it at naptime instead of at night."

This was bullshit—*we* didn't do naptime, *I* did, and of course nap or night wouldn't matter, the point was he needed the binky to fall asleep—but I didn't say so. I called bullshit all the time before the baby, but that was another thing that changed once I stopped working. I felt less confident about things, and for some reason it seemed more likely that I'd be wrong instead of right.

On Monday morning I kind of hoped again that Harold would forget, but after he kissed us goodbye, he wished us both luck. "This is the day, buddy! Who's a big boy? *You* are!" He poked Hal in the chest and made a pop-pop noise, and the baby cackled and grabbed his father's finger. *Stop it, that hurts.*

The morning went by too fast. After lunch I tried to keep Hal awake, but I knew it wouldn't work and eventually I had to put him down in the crib. *See you after!* He grabbed up the pacifier and started sucking, and I waited until his eyelids were half-shut before I left the room. I took up my book of stories and tried to read, but it was impossible to concentrate.

When I knew he'd be asleep I went to the kitchen, cursing Drew and his wife and, okay, my husband too for thinking their way was the best. I plucked the scissors out of the drawer, listened for any sounds before creeping to the crib, and picked up the pacifier from where it had dropped next to Hal's cheek. It was all I could do not to make a noise when I cut it down the middle; I felt the snip inside my chest. I laid the binky's severed halves on the sheet and left the door open a crack behind me. The pair of scissors I shoved back in its drawer, like something I hated (it was), then forced myself to sit on the couch instead of jumping up to run to my bureau, where I'd hidden an identical pacifier it would have been easy to swap in for the useless fragments before Hal woke up.

I read somewhere that babies start out thinking they have two mothers: the one who cuddles and gives them what they want, and the one who's on the phone too long or late with the bottle or in some other way falls down on the job. At some point they realize that this spectrum exists in a single person—the one and only mother they're stuck with—and then, watch out! Tiny minds blown.

I was hoping Hal hadn't reached that point yet. I was hoping we could both blame the bad mommy for what I'd just done.

The minute I heard him stir, I hopped up and peeked through the crack to see him sitting in the crib and slapping around on the sheet. He picked up the first binky piece and stared at it, then saw the second part and picked it up, too. He tried to fit the two pieces together as if he thought they might click into place, like the jigsaw we'd been doing of a dinosaur.

He had some words by now, and pretty soon he'd be able to say whatever he wanted; I wouldn't have to interpret what I saw behind his eyes. When the rubber pieces fell out of his hands in front of him, he bent over a little and asked, as if the fragments themselves might answer, "Broken?"

You cut the damn thing while he's sleeping, Drew had explained to Harold. *Boom, no more binky! But it will just be something that happened, not something you did.*

I could see how this might work. After all, Harold had pronounced it brilliant.

But *you* try destroying something your baby loves, and see how brilliant it is.

I snatched him out of the crib faster than usual and rushed to put on his favorite show, which I never did after a nap, and the novelty of this succeeded in distracting him. Maybe it *would* be this easy, I thought—maybe when he woke up, he'd looked down at the love object that had somehow been rendered unusable while he slept, and made peace with the sad truth.

But that night, when he began squalling as soon as we put him down, I realized he'd just been in shock at the sight of the broken binky. Harold wanted to close our bedroom door, but I asked him not to. "Punishing yourself?" he asked, and I said No, I just wanted to hear what was going on in there, even though once I thought about it I realized he was right.

I hadn't planned to show him the replacement pacifier still in its packaging, but I did, because I knew he'd discourage me from ripping it out of the plastic and rushing it to the crib. "But that defeats the whole purpose," Harold said. The tone in his voice was the same one I might have heard if I'd told him I thought it would be a good idea to start feeding Hal popcorn for breakfast.

He asked me why on earth I'd bought another pacifier, when the whole idea was to get rid of the one we already had. I said it was just in case.

"Just in case what?

I couldn't answer. I just shook my head. If he had to ask, I knew no amount of explaining would make him understand.

"That's messed up, Nia," he said. "You know that, right?"

This time I nodded, but not because I thought it was messed up. I nodded because he expected me to.

Do I need to mention that I didn't go back to work after Hal's next birthday? I'm sure I don't. We moved into a house of our own and I had another baby instead, the girl who came before the second boy. Harold proposed binkies for both of them, but I said they could use their thumbs instead. How pathetic is it that it felt like a victory each time he gave in to me? As pathetic as it gets, I am aware.

That night, with Harold in the bathroom, I left the new pacifier behind and went to stand at the foot of Hal's crib. He must have sensed my presence, because he stopped wailing and pulled himself up to a stand across from me. *It was you, wasn't it? If it was you, don't tell me.* I put a hand out to touch his cheek, and he put his own hand up to hold mine there. A moment he'll never remember and I'll never forget.

I wish you hadn't done that. That's when I knew it had been my own voice, not his, telling me things all along. And as soon as I understood this, I stopped being able to hear it at all.

An Interest in History

I went for a walk on the trail at a park not far from where I lived. I was desperate for somebody to look me in the eye, and I figured a stranger was better than no one.

It wasn't just any trail, or any park, but the Minute Man national historic site commemorating the first battles of the Revolution. A couple of British soldiers are buried at North Bridge. I liked to go there for perspective, when I needed a reminder that my own life was not all that dramatic or dire.

I'd been banished from my job, and the feeling of it carried over to everything else. I was free to go anywhere other than the federal building downtown where I'd worked, but being legally prohibited from entering one public space made me feel like an outcast in all of them. I went a day and a half without leaving my apartment, feeling stung, before it occurred to me that maybe I was making a bigger deal out of all this than it actually was.

Do one thing every day that scares you, Eleanor Roosevelt said. Today, this was my thing.

I put on jeans and a sweatshirt and drove to the park. It was ten-thirty on a Wednesday morning, not too crowded, most of us women. A few runners, a few walking pairs. I put my hood on and started out. It was a warm day for October, and after a hundred yards or so I pulled the hood away. No one would recognize me here—right? Of course they wouldn't. I was thirty miles from the scene of what I'd been accused of, and the people who had accused me were all at work. I should be safe, I thought, to enjoy some exercise in the fresh fall air, the colors on the trees along the path, and the pleasure of making eye contact with someone—anyone—after going too long without.

I passed plenty of people, but (and this is what I'd been afraid of) not one of them looked me in the eye.

It had been a while since I'd taken a walk like this, out in nature, so I thought maybe I was just rusty. Maybe *I* wasn't doing a good job of indicating my willingness to acknowledge my trail-mates, and to exchange pleasantries as we passed. I'm aware that "exchanging pleasantries" is a cliché, but the truth is that I wasn't looking for anything extraordinary or original. What I really wanted more than anything was just to smile and nod at another human being, and receive a smile and nod in return.

So I made a point of trying. With everyone I saw coming toward me, I smiled as I approached, and sought to meet their eyes. Nothing. After a few failures, I even cleared my throat and closed the gap between us on the trail, but this only caused them to move and look away farther.

Of course I considered the possibility, as I had when I first noticed this pattern, that it was something about *me* causing people to avert their gaze from mine. But observing others on the trail, I watched the same thing happen every time, between strangers crossing paths.

Was it only because I had an interest in history that I wanted things to go back to the way they used to be, when people looked at each other? That couldn't be it, I decided. It couldn't be just me.

I drove home feeling more shaken than when I had left, and stopped in at the mailroom before heading up to my apartment. A woman I'd noticed before, but never spoken to, was crouched in front of her own box at the end of the row. Her baby sat in its stroller, facing me as I pulled out my mail, and when I dared to look into his wide eyes above the pacifier he sucked with such happiness, I saw to my shock and pleasure that he was looking back at me. It struck me so hard I nearly gasped, though I was careful not to do so because I knew it would call his mother to him, and then the baby would look at *her*.

The thrill of it! I understood suddenly how that phrase originated, "catching someone's glance." You throw and they catch, or the opposite, but either way it's a transaction that benefits both. *Bless you, baby*, I thought.

The agency summoned me back to the office the next day, for a meeting. They were trying to get to the bottom of things. Why I'd done what I did, give out information I wasn't supposed to, to someone who wasn't supposed to have it. Not "compromise the integrity of the agency," which was the way they put it—that's not what I had done.

I tried to explain that it was a matter of intimacy, of trying to connect. The person I'd been sitting with, on the night in question, was someone I considered a friend. Leaning closer over our dinner plates to ask me for details, she looked me in the eye with such interest and investment that I almost started to weep. This was the closest I'd felt to anyone in months. Years? A seduction it felt like, almost—I would have said anything to keep her eyes on mine. It never occurred to me that it might backfire. That she'd take what I told her and use it against me as she did.

The people conducting the investigation—my bosses, whom I'd also considered friends—shifted in their seats across the table as if they couldn't believe what they were hearing. "Don't you get how this sounds, Natalie?" one of them asked. "It's as if you've lost sight entirely of what we do here. Of the need for discretion. Of the agreement you signed when you came to work for us."

I said, "You don't understand how it happened?" It was not a response to his question, I realized. "Haven't you noticed that nobody looks anyone in the eye anymore?"

Of course, none of them answered. What could they have said—*No*? It would have been recognized for the lie it was.

"I think I see the problem," the HR representative said. She was a delicate speaker and mover, someone who got people to tell her their secrets even if they'd promised themselves they would not. "Maybe we could arrange some counseling, and after that, reassess where we stand?"

My bosses were all frowning, looking down at their phones and their legal pads. But they agreed to leave me alone with the HR woman, to see what could be worked out.

"I think the problem is that you're more sensitive than other people," she told me, once they'd cleared the room. "And I'm sure that can be an asset, but it's not serving you right now. With this particular… obsession you seem to have."

"I wouldn't call it an obsession. Are you saying you haven't noticed it, yourself? That people don't ever look you in the eye?" I moved my head forward slightly in an effort to catch her glance, but she was scribbling notes in my employment file.

"No, I'm not saying that. Of course I've noticed. But it's just the way things are now. People are overwhelmed. They have a lot on their minds. It's not like the old days, when you'd walk down the road in your petticoat and stop to pass the time of day with whoever happened to come along."

Petticoat! The word made both of us smile, though not at each other the way it should have been.

"It's not just about eye contact," I said. How was I ever going to get someone to understand? "Do you know anything about President Garfield's assassination?" She shook her head, and I chose to ignore my impression that she'd never heard of a President Garfield. "When the funeral train was transporting him to his house, people all along the route laid down flowers and straw on the tracks, to make the ride softer. For a dead man! Talk about paying respect. Can you imagine anything like that happening today?"

Now I had her attention, I saw. She met my eyes for the briefest instant—there came that thrill, again—and I could tell she was imagining the scene. "Yes, that *is* poignant," she murmured. Then she seemed to shake herself out of whatever reverie my story had cast on her. "But there's always been bad people and good people. Rude people and polite ones. It's nothing new."

I told her I agreed. I reminded her of the Eleanor Roosevelt quote that even in our blackest moments, we have to acknowledge that there is something very fine in human beings.

Then I asked, "When did it happen, the whole not-looking-in-the-eye thing? I missed the moment. It just seems like one day they did, and the next day they didn't."

The HR person declined to respond right away. I could tell she was sizing me up somehow, and the situation. As she did so, she focused on the filing cabinet in a corner of the room.

"I think I can save your job," she said finally. "But you'll be on probation, and you have to promise never to do anything like this again. It wouldn't be three strikes and you're out—the second one would be the boot. And I can't promise that the next time they won't press charges, or take some other action you really don't want to face."

It was a hard choice. But I knew what I had to say. I'd be giving up a good job with a chance for advancement, and great benefits, but if nobody was going to meet my eyes when we passed in the hall or sat across from each other at the conference table, what was the point? It wasn't worth it. I told the HR woman this, and I sensed she was disappointed. It touched me that this might be for my own sake, more than the agency's, but at the same time she was looking down at my file rather than into my eyes when I saw this expression on her face, so I knew I'd made the right decision.

I took a couple of weeks off, during which I went for walks at Minute Man, and at the end of my "vacation" I saw a notice on the bulletin board of the Visitors Center that they were looking for someone to work behind the desk. I applied and got the job, even though at first they were suspicious because I was overqualified. But I told them a version of the truth—that my position at the state agency was too impersonal, and that I would relish the opportunity to greet the public and welcome them to the park.

All of this occurred a year or so ago. Do I miss my high-level job, and the agency? Well, yes. It wasn't easy losing that status, not to mention the salary.

But was leaving the right thing to do? Also yes. When people approach my desk at the Visitors Center, to ask about the location of the shot heard 'round the world or the site of Paul Revere's capture, I wait a few seconds before looking up to answer. That way, I know they will have stopped looking at their phone or stopped yapping at their children, and I will enjoy their complete focus because they want something from me. (For that is the sad secret, I've come to see.) I look them in the eye and smile, and they look and smile back. Sometimes we exchange pleasantries before getting down to business. Sometimes we don't. Either way is okay with me, because I've gotten the nourishment I need.

Yesterday, a girl of middle-school age stood by the lobby's front door, waiting I assumed for a parent to pick her up. She called over to ask me what time the center closed, but did not raise her eyes from her phone when I smiled and called back the answer. Had she been here with the school group? I asked, coming around the side of my desk so we'd be closer to each other and not have to shout. Had she missed the bus?

She shook her head without looking up. Her hair fell across both eyes, though she must have been able to see through it because she moved her thumbs quickly across the screen. Oh, I remember the agony of being thirteen, and I wished so much to express this to her with understanding in my eyes. But of course she wasn't looking, so instead I asked if she'd enjoyed her visit. She nodded again, though barely.

I took a few more steps until I stood next to her, and put a hand on her slumped shoulder as I said, "Look at me." I had never been explicitly prohibited from touching a guest, though come to think of it, I don't remember if the subject ever came up.

She jumped as if a cat had leapt on her without warning. "Get *away* from me," she exclaimed, and I retreated, not fully understanding that I'd made a mistake. "What's the matter with you?"

This close, I could hear the audio of what she'd been watching—some video about a competition involving maple syrup and guinea pigs. If Paul Revere could have known!

"I was just trying to get your attention," I told the girl gently, feeling how urgent it was to warn her. "I know your generation isn't used to looking people in the eye. A lot of older people have stopped doing it, too. But trust me, it's a habit you want to break while you still can. I'm saying this for your own good. Try connecting with an actual person, instead of just through a screen."

She didn't answer, but took several big, conspicuous steps away from me to the other side of the lobby. A car pulled up and she hurried outside to enter it, and I watched her lean forward to say something to the woman driving, with a gesture in my direction. The woman peered out beyond her daughter, but by that point I'd retreated, and I don't know if she saw me or not.

I'm being called in again, and it would be a lie to say I'm not nervous. I love this job and I need it, and I don't know what I'll do if I get the boot.

But I won't back down if it comes to that. This feels bigger than me now. To quote Mrs. Roosevelt again, the future belongs to those who believe in the beauty of their dreams. We all want the same thing, I'm sure of it—it's just that most people have given up, or they don't know how to go about fixing what's been wrong for too long. Or they're overwhelmed, like the HR woman said. I know I'm just one person and it might not make a difference, but I'll keep trying, because who knows? Somebody has to see the threat for what it is, and do something. Somebody has to take a stand.

Take What You Want

My father composed his note on the back of the last shopping list my mother ever wrote. She left it on the counter without making it to the store, and I threw it away when I was cleaning the house so people could come over after the funeral. But my father fished it out of the trash and jotted down what he wanted.

In cleaning the house, I decided to use my mother's method, which was to do a task, then reward myself with a chapter from whatever I was reading. This is how I grew up, watching her dust or vacuum a room and then settle down with a book.

Usually I went in for fiction that made me feel and think. I could stand the sad stuff. But right after my mother died, all I wanted was romance and fantasy. I'd be an old woman before the library ran out of those.

My father's note said, "I and my children would like to thank the construction workers at the Glenville roundabout for the respect they showed as the hurst went by them. They all removed there helmets and bent heads as we past by. Thank you very much from the family of Constance Lin."

He handed it to me. I read it and must have made a face without realizing. "What?" he said.

My mother would have been embarrassed by the mistakes. But pointing them out would embarrass my father, and he was the one between them who could still feel anything. I considered asking, "Do you want me to edit it for you?" since that's my line of work, but then I remembered how after the funeral, my brother had taken over as host in the receiving line, even though my father stood first. I knew my brother believed he was helping, saving Dad from having to spend a lot of energy on other people, but the whole time our father just looked confused, then hurt, then tired. Not angry—never angry, no matter how much it would have been the right thing for him to feel. My mother always had enough of that for the two of them. I figured it was probably what killed her, all that anger building up inside until there was no place for it to go, but I was afraid to ask anyone in my family if they thought this, too.

"Nothing," I said to my father. "Just, you know, it's painful."

He nodded. "You and me both."

I'd sat between him and my brother in the car behind the hearse when we went through the rotary. Our father was the one who noticed first what the construction workers were doing, and he pointed it out to us. I cried a little, and Doug whispered that I was a wuss.

"Very classy," my father murmured. He'd raised a hand against the window to acknowledge the workers' gesture, though they wouldn't have seen it because their heads were bowed. "She would really have liked that."

I posted my father's note to our community's social media website, and it got a lot of thumbs up. My brother drove back to Columbus the next day. I told my father I'd stay for a week or two, to help him sort out Mom's things and get used to being without her. He smiled, and I appreciated his not pointing out what a silly thing I had said.

"What about work?" he asked then. "They can do without you?"

I explained that they wouldn't be doing without me—that I'd be able to do most of my assignments remotely, and the others could wait. He seemed to think it meant something about how important I was, that I had this option, and I'm ashamed to say I didn't correct him.

YOU THINK IT'S NEVER GOING TO END—the reaching into drawers and closets and cupboards, pulling out items to set on the floor or the counter or the bed, before deciding which pile to put them in. So hard to choose, because of the memories. *Will I regret it if I give that up? Will I wish I had it back?*

But it does end. An infinite number of feelings, but a finite number of things.

Among my mother's belongings, I didn't find any secrets. But then, I hadn't expected to. I wouldn't have offered to do the job if I hadn't figured on what I would find.

I both didn't want to be there and didn't want to leave. My father both could and could not take care of himself. I didn't have to cook much because of all the condolence casseroles, but I kept the house neat, and every day at lunchtime I went to the grocery store. I didn't have to—the fridge was full—but I liked going because the house was so quiet, with my father back at work, that I thought I might go nuts otherwise. Kroger was bright and ordinary and filled with people. It gave me something normal and productive and easy to do.

A week and a half after the funeral, in the checkout line, I ran into Mark Spilka. We both used to spend our lunch hour in the school library instead of the cafeteria; there were two big easy chairs next to a fake mantel above a fake fireplace, and in this way we ended up sitting next to each other even though we wouldn't have chosen to do so otherwise. I read books and he wrote them, scribbling fast in a Star Trek notebook and sometimes giggling out loud, amusing himself (or at least, that's how it seemed to me) with his own genius. Sometimes he read a line out loud to me, and I have to admit he was good; I recognized it even then.

He wrote less about what happened than about the people it happened to, and this intrigued me. There was more to him than what we all saw, I remember thinking, and I also remember thinking that this was profound of me. I said he should let me read his stories someday, and he said, "In a few years you can pay for them like everyone else," and I laughed, and he looked insulted.

He was a funny mix, both a brain and a burnout, which fascinated me because I thought you had to choose. Everyone *else* seemed to have to choose.

The only actual class we took together was an English elective, Song Lyrics as Poetry, taught by a short but otherwise enormous woman named Ms. Bello. She was young and pretty, but of course the only thing most people noticed about her was that she was fat.

I had never heard any Joni Mitchell before that class, or Judy Collins or Carole King. It was the best class I ever took and the only one I remember. I still can't hear *Both Sides Now* without feeling the hard sting of the tears I tried to hold back when Ms. Bello played the song and I sat at my desk staring down at my binder, where someone had scribbled "Eat me" when I wasn't looking.

At Kroger, Mark was ahead of me in the line. He said he'd seen that my mother had died, and told me he was sorry. I asked if he'd ended up writing the Great American Novel, and he said, "Still working on it," which I thought was kind of cheeky until I realized he was making fun of himself.

He asked what I was doing with my life, and I described my job at the academic publishing house, making it sound more interesting and important than it actually was. He said, "That's not what I meant, but okay," and I remembered how much power he'd always had to make me feel stupid.

On top of being a brain and a burnout, Mark had also been mean. One day we were all sitting in the classroom waiting for Ms. Bello, and he and this other burnout Brian cued up the sound system so that "Fat Bottomed Girls" began playing right as she came in. Ms. Bello turned dark red and tried to smile as she reminded us all that she was a woman, not a girl, and it would serve us later in life if we bothered now to learn the distinction.

At Kroger Mark waited for me to check out, even though it took a while, and as we exited the store he said we should grab a drink. I was flustered: was Mark Spilka asking me out? "Right now?" I said, and he said no, he had to go back to work, but he'd be at The Bitter End after dinner if I wanted to meet him.

I didn't tell my father I was going on a date, both because I didn't know if that's what it was and because I didn't want him to think I was being disrespectful to our family's grief. I told him I was meeting up with an old friend from high school who needed some editing help, and he asked who it was and I made up a name, and he said, "Good for you, honey. You can't let all this consume you."

It wasn't consuming me, which I felt guilty about. But there was no point in saying so.

I kept telling myself it didn't matter what I wore to meet Mark, which is why I got so aggravated trying on three shirts before I settled, not all that happily, on a fourth. But I tried to let go of it as I drove the short distance to the bar. He was waiting for me outside, and I appreciated his guessing that I preferred not to walk in alone. He asked what I wanted and though what I wanted was a vodka tonic, I said Coke because I didn't want to let my guard down around him. He went to the bar and came back with my drink and a glass of beer, which he made a point of telling me was alcohol-free. When I raised my eyebrows he said, "Yeah, I'm sober. Booze and pot both, almost two years."

I congratulated him then blushed, not sure if that was appropriate or not, but he seemed to appreciate it. We talked a little about high school, and I asked if he remembered that day with Ms. Bello and the song he and Brian had blasted when she entered the room. However Mark answered, I thought, would tell me what I needed to know about which kind of person he'd turned out to be.

He winced and looked down at the floor. "Yeah. Of course. I was an asshole back then. The drugs didn't help, but I can't blame it on that."

I felt my stomach unclench a little. "How'd she die, anyway? I only found out about it later."

Did I really want to hear the answer? The truth was, I was afraid of it. But I also needed to know.

Mark shrugged, but not in a way that said it didn't matter. "I never really heard anything specific. I just figured a heart attack or something—all that extra weight." He took a long swig of his Bud Zero. "I wish she was still alive, so I could go back and make amends."

When he said that, I realized I felt the same way about my mother. It was a jolt—so simple, so true, yet it hadn't occurred to me before that.

And yet, I thought, amends for what?

It was my turn to say something, but my brain went blank. I might as well have ordered the vodka, after all. Mark seemed to pick up on this, and I felt grateful that he took it upon himself to keep the conversation going. "Bello was cool, though. Coming up with that save about being a woman instead of a girl. I mean, not exactly a *save*. She was pretty crushed. But you know what I mean."

I nodded. Until he said "crushed" I hadn't remembered exactly how our teacher had looked, when she realized that everybody understood the Fat Bottom song was directed at her. To change the subject I asked Mark where he worked, and he told me Home Depot. I must have looked surprised, because he said, "I know. Underachieving. But I'm working on it."

Again he waited for me to say something, and again when I didn't, he filled in. "So listen, it wasn't an accident, running into you earlier. I get my lunch at Kroger every day, and I saw you a couple of times there already."

Well, if he meant to distract me from the image of Ms. Bello being humiliated, it worked. "You mean, as in stalking?" Right away I regretted implying that I thought I was somebody worthy of being stalked.

"I wouldn't call it that," Mark said. He smiled. "More like working up my nerve."

Was he trying, now, to humiliate *me*? I dared to look at him straight on, not taking my eyes away until I believed he might have meant what he said. This flustered me more than being humiliated, which I would have known how to deal with.

Mark lowered his voice and leaned forward. "I read your father's note on the community board. I saw you were the one who posted it, so I knew you saw the mistakes and didn't fix them. I thought, That says something about you. And then when I saw you the second time in Kroger, I wanted to know what it was."

I sat back in my chair. I hadn't realized, before now, how much I'd wanted to talk to someone about how I felt posting that note.

"And I know you probably won't believe me," Mark went on, "but those times in the library, during lunch? That was my favorite part of the day. I just couldn't tell you back then. So when I saw you were home, I figured why not take a flyer and see where it lands?"

The line sounded glib, and I wondered if he'd practiced or at least planned it. "Well," I said, hearing the word come out in a whisper. I made myself sit up straighter and summoned my voice. "I appreciate that."

He seemed to sense that I felt uncomfortable, and I was glad when he smiled again. It was a different smile from the one I was used to seeing on him, and it made me feel a different way. "It was sweet, what those construction workers did in the rotary. Showing respect for your mom." He finished his Bud Zero and signaled for another. "She would have liked that."

I squinted at him. "What do you mean? You didn't know my mother."

A beat passed before he said, "No, but I mean *anybody* would like it, right? That kind of thing happening when the procession passes through."

I said I guessed so, and looked down at the table. It was all kind of surreal by that point, I admit. Sitting across from Mark Spilka at The Bitter End, feeling that little shock when I said the words "my mother" because they were always followed by the moment of remembering she didn't exist anymore.

"Actually," Mark said, and when I looked up again, he had what I'd call a sheepish expression on his face—something I'd never imagined seeing there. "Since you bring it up, I *did* know your mom. A little."

"You did? How?" I couldn't imagine any reason for my mother to go to Home Depot. Anything you could buy there would be my father's department.

"We went to meetings together." Mark closed his fist around the new glass set down in front of him. "I mean, we didn't *go* to them together. But I saw her there."

"What kind of meeting?" I both knew and didn't know. I understood what kind of meeting Mark had to go to. But what he said about my mother also being there made no sense.

He told me she'd begun appearing at his regular "nooner" two months ago. I laughed, remembered who was sitting across from me, then said, "I don't even know why you'd think that was funny."

He frowned. "I wouldn't joke about something like this."

"You're trying to make me believe my mother said she was an alcoholic?" I pronounced the word with more derision than I would have, if I'd been thinking about it. "She was practically a teetotaler. Her father drank too much, and she never wanted to be like him."

Now Mark nodded, as if he'd already known all this. It was infuriating. "She did it in secret," he said. "Like a lot of us do."

"That's impossible. She couldn't have hidden that from us."

Yet even as I said it I realized that yes, she could have. My brother and I both lived hours—states—away, now. She could have begun drinking in the house when she was alone, or at her job in the town clerk's office, and she could also have started going to meetings at noon, on her lunch hour, without anyone knowing. Our father was busy at the plant all day, and even when he was home, he'd never been big on noticing things. Once, my mother had a skin biopsy and came home with a bandage over the spot above her lip. She had to leave the bandage on for a day. She told me later, seeming amused, that my father never mentioned it.

But I don't think she took this as a sign that he didn't love her, and I didn't, either. It seemed more as if he just took his family for granted, which, to be honest, I don't see anything wrong with. Isn't that what families are for?

I reached for the lime in my Coke and squeezed it as hard as I could. "Come on," I said to Mark. "You're fucking with me, right?"

He shook his head. "No, Steph. I wouldn't. I mean it."

"Because that's really fucked up, you know. She just died. My mother just *died*."

"I know that." He said it in almost a whisper. "I know she did. I'm sorry." He shifted in his seat. "I think she was getting ready to tell you all. She was pretty sure none of you knew, including your father. That she drank, and that she got sober. It was eating her up, both those things. She was going to write you and Dougie letters, and tell your father in person. But then what happened happened. She never got the chance."

There was music playing somewhere; it felt loud and hot in my head. My mother was the only one who ever called Doug *Dougie*. Mark arranged his hands on the table into some sort of figure—a heart, maybe, or maybe it was a knot. I couldn't tell from where I sat. The expression on his face was one I'd never seen there before: Mark Spilka doubted himself. It might have made me feel sicker than anything else, even more absurd and unlikely than what he'd told me about my mother, which I didn't believe.

I didn't say so, though. I didn't say anything. My silence made things awkward, and Mark kept talking. "Listen, Steph, I really shouldn't be saying any of this. Not that I can do anything about it now, but I'm having second thoughts about telling you. I just thought you should know, and I thought she'd *want* you to know. Technically, it was wrong of me." He fidgeted, waiting for me again to say something. Instead I reached across the table and took a big gulp of his non-alcoholic beer.

What had I thought, or hoped? That it was not a Bud Zero after all, and that I'd feel alcohol rushing to my blood, a sign that everything he told me was bullshit?

Mark managed not to look surprised. Maybe he understood right away why I'd done it. I said, "I don't suppose you have any proof of this, or anything? About my mother?"

"Proof?" He held both palms up as if to say, *Who, me?* "What kind of proof?"

"I don't know. Texts. Something. Whatever."

"Why are you asking me that?"

"Because I don't believe you." This time I wasn't the first to look away. It was a dare to myself; if I held on longer than he did, maybe that would mean I was right.

The smile disappeared and he sat back slowly, as if afraid he might injure himself if he wasn't careful. "So you think I could have made all this up, and asked you out so I could tell you a cruel lie? Why would I do that? Why would anyone?"

"I don't know. Just to hurt people." I pointed at him. "You're Mark Spilka. You tell *me*."

He flinched, then studied me for another long moment before he said, "I'm not lying, Steph. But I can't force you to believe me. We have this saying in the program—because not everything works for everybody—'Take what you want and leave the rest.'"

"Yeah, well." I snorted. "I'm leaving *all* of it. You haven't changed one bit."

He had a decision to make. I saw the struggle behind his eyes. If he'd made a different one, would it have been better for both of us? At least it would have been better for him—I knew it then and I know it now, to the extent that I let myself think about that moment.

But what he did was give me the smile I remembered from high school. "So what do you think, Stephanie?" he said, and here came a chill from the way he pronounced my full name, drawing the syllables out. "About Fat Bottom Bello. Did they have to use hydraulics to get her into the *hurst*, or what?"

I gasped, and stood up so quickly without planning it that my chair fell over backward, causing a clatter that made everyone in the bar turn to look at us. "You're still an asshole," I told him. It was not a word I said often, and it came out softer than the others, but it was clear he heard it. "I thought sober people were supposed to be... not assholes."

He pointed at me as if to say, *Right. Gotcha!* But I saw his hand shaking.

When I got home my father was sitting in my mother's favorite chair, tuned in to her favorite crime series. She'd loved watching people figure things out, and she loved seeing bad guys get theirs. My father turned the volume down and remarked that I was home early, and I said it had been an easy job, the one my friend had asked for help with.

I went into the kitchen and poured a glass of water, then drank it as I looked through the window into the night. It was so dark I couldn't make out anything in the yard: the tool shed, the bird feeders, the swing set my parents kept saying it was about time to take down. How many hours had my mother spent doing just this—looking through this same window, but not actually seeing anything? Taking for granted she knew what was there?

I'm still embarrassed to admit what bothered me more than that, though. It was the idea that I'd thought Mark Spilka could be interested in a date with me, when it turned out he probably only wanted to stir things up. Cause trouble. Take a flyer and see where it landed—his favorite time had been in the library with me, my ass.

But I couldn't be sure. Which Mark Spilka had told me those things about himself and about my mother? Who had my mother been, and had I known her or not?

I went back and watched the rest of the show with my father. At the end, I said that my boss had called, and it turned out they needed me back after all. He nodded and told me how much he appreciated my having stayed so long, how he couldn't have gotten through it without me. "Almost like having her around," he said, his voice catching a little. Then he made me promise that if I ever needed anything, I'd be sure to let him know.

Infusion

I was the one who brought my mother to the rheumatology center for her final infusion. There'd been four of them, four weeks in a row, and my sister and brother had taken care of the first three. We figured it was fair because the last appointment would be the longest. Well, not exactly *fair*, because my sister covered two of the earlier days and my brother only one, but nobody expects any different when it comes to adult children helping their parents in their old age. My mother had been told numerous times, by her friends and even the doctors themselves when it became clear she'd need so many medical visits, how lucky she was to have two daughters. In fact, I'm pretty sure that's the only reason my brother volunteered to do the one day—because he was so sick of hearing that story.

But between my sister and me, it seemed fair, not only because my appointment was longer, but because this kind of thing is harder on me than it is on her. She lives closer to our mother; she minds less than I do driving to unfamiliar places; and she doesn't obsess as much about worst-case scenarios, which is my specialty. Even when the date was still four weeks away, I began imagining an accident on the way to the rheumatologist's, and getting lost, and oversleeping so that we'd be late for the appointment scheduled to begin at ten a.m. Never mind that I haven't slept past six o'clock since I was in college, or that my body always wakes me up early when I have an important morning obligation. During that whole month, I lived in more dread than usual.

On top of all that, it's hard for me to wear a mask for long periods. It makes me feel claustrophobic and kind of panicky. But of course, you had to wear a mask the whole time in the medical office.

We wouldn't know if the infusions worked until after the lab tests they would run on our mother the following week. We were all hopeful, but she was seventy-five, after all, and the disease had done a number on her before it was even diagnosed. The past two years since the first lockdown had been hard on her, living alone and then getting all these strange symptoms that kept her from doing the things she could have done even with the restrictions—meeting friends for lunches outside, going for walks. She'd grown frail, in her body and her spirit, and it was hard to tell how far she might return after these treatments.

Our mother herself seemed to need to believe that after this fourth infusion, she'd be all better, and could simply pick up with the life she had before. None of the three of us did anything to dissuade her from this conviction. If positive thinking was going to have anything to do with her outcome, we wanted as much as possible of it on board.

It rained the morning of the final treatment, and an ice storm was forecast for later that day. My mother was afraid for us to go out in it, and I admit I was tempted to give in to her inclination to reschedule, but I knew it would upset my siblings and besides, the air wasn't supposed to start freezing until after we got back to my mother's. So, I put on a cheerful attitude I didn't actually feel, and off we went. My mother was nervous, I could tell. She kept thanking me, and praising my driving. *I've been driving for thirty years!* I wanted to remind her, but I didn't because frankly, I'd rather not be reminded of this myself. Anyway, I just took it slow in the rain. A couple of cars honked at me as they passed, pissing me off, but I held in the curses I would have shouted if I'd been alone. We made it to the rheumatology center with no missed turns or accidents. Of course, it wasn't as bad as I thought it would be. Hardly anything ever is.

I'm always early, so we had a few minutes to kill. We sat on the couch in a corner of the waiting room, which the receptionist had told us was unofficially reserved for people accompanying patients to long infusions. "Did you bring something to do for all that time?" my mother asked, and I told her I had a book with me, not to worry.

"But I do," she said, and I knew it was the truth. Here she was getting infusions for a disease that was tearing down her immune system, and she was worried about *me*.

Charles, the technician, came out to fetch my mother for her treatment. He wore a mask that said *I Was Social Distancing Before It Was Cool*. My sister and brother had already met him, and my sister referred to him as Charles in Charge. "This is my daughter Sheila," my mother said. She'd always pronounced my name, and my brother's and sister's, as if we were the only people in the world who had the names we did.

"Be good," my mother told me, then laughed and added, "Oh, that was a silly thing to say. Of course you'll be good."

She'd lost a lot of weight in the last year, and her smile scared me because it resembled a ghost's. At the same time, I was happy to see it. I gave her a hug, and I could see that both she and Charles were touched by this. My mother's hug back, you would not have believed. She was a lot weaker now than she'd ever been, but she hugged me so hard it almost hurt—though at the same time, it woke up an old feeling of safety I'd thought was gone forever. "We'll try to bring her back to you in one piece," Charles told me, leading her off. I knew from my brother and sister that he'd said the same thing during each of the previous three visits.

I settled myself on the couch and tried to read the mystery I'd brought with me, but I found it hard to care about. Who cared? Not me. I remembered then that there's something about medical offices that makes you see everything differently. The list of things you thought were important melts down to just one or two. After a while I put the book back in my bag and just sat on the couch, which was surprisingly comfortable, and looked out at the rain.

For the first hour I just sat there with my own thoughts, a habit I tried but failed to cultivate in my own kids. "I know you don't believe this," I remember telling Chloe shortly before she left for college, "but trust me, there'll come a time when you won't have your phone or the TV or another person to distract you, and it's just going to be you alone with your own mind. And if you're not used to it, that can be... unsettling."

Chloe responded with the smirk she'd practiced all summer. "And when is this going to happen, Mom? Am I being sent to Siberia and nobody told me? Did you sign me up for a vacation on the moon?"

I only smiled and let her think she'd won, because as good an idea as it seemed when I brought it up, suddenly I didn't want my daughter to understand the loneliness I was describing. She'd find out on her own the same way I had, the same way everyone else in the world does. What was the hurry? Let her enjoy the ignorance as long as she could.

At the infusion center, people came in and out both sets of doors—the ones leading to the waiting room from outside, and the ones separating the waiting room from what my sister called the inner sanctum, where the treatments were administered. Many were simple injections, my mother had told me. The receptionist behind the front desk would slide aside the partition, greet each new patient with warm eyes and a smile she made visible even through her mask, pass a few lines of chitchat, hand over the clipboard containing the questionnaire about symptoms, then slide the partition shut again while the patient sat down to fill it out.

The staff behind the desk were nervous about the freezing rain coming, and their commutes home. I heard them talking about it. But still they turned bright faces to the patients coming in to get treated, offering them some cheer. It gave a nudge to my heart, if it isn't too corny to say so. That's just the truth.

A couple about my own age entered, under an umbrella so big it might as well have been a tent. The woman shook it out in the foyer, then stood behind her husband as they approached the desk, which was how I knew he was the patient. He took the clipboard the receptionist gave him and handed it to his wife as they sat down across from me. She began reading the symptoms off one by one. I couldn't tell whether he was unable because of his condition to make out the words on the page, or if this was just the way they did things.

"Blurred vision?" she asked.

"No," he said.

"Nausea?"

"No."

"Vomiting?"

"No."

She paused for just the slightest moment before continuing. "Anxiety."

"Yes," the man said, also after a slight pause.

"Depression."

"Yes."

The wife gave a small nod. She'd been checking each box before her husband responded. She looked a little younger than him, and she was more put-together: stylish, and with better posture. But he was a sick person, after all. He was bald and a little shlumpy and wore an old Yankees shirt. Had she encouraged him to dress up a little more for his appointment?

She wouldn't have suggested it for the doctor's sake, but for her husband himself. *It'll make you feel better*, she'd have said. But maybe they were long beyond that by now.

A different technician came out to get him. The wife and I looked at each other, and I think we both smiled. Then she took yarn and needles out of her purse and began to knit.

I wondered if she thought I was here with a husband, too. If she'd asked, I would have told her that mine was back home working and holding down the fort, though holding down the fort was not nearly as big a job now as it used to be when the kids lived there. Now, it mainly meant feeding the cats.

I was feeling cranky, I admit. We'd had a fight just before I left to drive to my mother's, and thinking about him stirred the dull sting of it in my heart. The argument was so small and stupid I barely remembered how it had started. There was so much less worth arguing about now than there was, before.

I still had three hours to go of sitting there watching the rain fall. I was worried it would turn to sleet by the time we started back, giving me a treacherous drive. I was cranky because my mother was sick and I knew that even if the infusions worked, she would still have this disease and she was seventy-five and no matter how hard she hoped, things were never going to go back to the way they'd been for her, or for any of us.

Was *cranky* the right word? Well, no.

The husband who was depressed and anxious emerged from the inner sanctum before his wife had even finished knitting a row. So, I guessed, a simple injection for him. She stood and put a hand on his shoulder and said, "Let's go celebrate." I had to turn my face away so she wouldn't see the tears above my mask, though probably she wouldn't have minded; she would have understood.

"Good luck," she told me, and I said, "Thank you, you too." It was too much and not anywhere near enough, at the same time.

I texted my brother and sister. *Halfway through. Exhausted already.*

My sister wrote back immediately. *I know, right??!* It was clear to me that she got what I was saying, and even though I knew it was only a little icon she tapped on her screen, it comforted me to see the little heart emoji she included with her response. My brother didn't give his thumbs-up until hours later, but that was okay. He did what he could.

Around twelve-thirty, I took out the snack bar I'd brought with me, pulled my mask to one side, and ate in small, surreptitious bites. I was afraid of being yelled at for having my mask off, but no one seemed to notice. A young man came in carrying a food delivery for the employees behind the desk. "Roscoe to the rescue!" he called out, and the receptionist who'd been greeting patients with such animation all morning stood up to slide the partition and take the bags he handed her.

"How are the roads?" she asked him. "They bad yet?"

"Nah. Not supposed to freeze till later. You'll be home by then." She made a fretful sound expressing doubt. "Don't worry, Deb," he told her, "I *got* ya. I put in a good word with the guy upstairs." He jerked his thumb toward the sky.

As he turned to leave, he did a doubletake at the couch in the corner, then winked at me. I winked back, but too late—he was already outside again and jumping into his car, where I could see bags and bags of lunch orders filling the back seat.

I replaced my mask, sat back, and felt my muscles unfold. It was easier, suddenly, to breathe. What was it that came over me in that moment, allowing me to relax? Having overheard that the roads were still all right, for one thing. But there was more. And it was nothing I'd been remotely expecting from this assignment, that's for sure.

I recognized it the same way I would have recognized a face that had brought me joy a long time ago—with a lift and lightness that spread like glory through my chest. A feeling that had been hard to find in myself or the world, since the invasion by fear and rage.

Love this was, all of it: Charles in Charge making his tired joke about returning the patient in one piece; the woman behind the glass greeting us all with a smile her mask couldn't hide; a wife taking her sad, sick husband to celebrate; my sister sending a digital heart. Finally, the young man rushing to feed all those hungry people, taking the time to wink at a worried woman with nothing to do but watch the rain fall and wait for her mother to be brought back to her.

Undefeated

"That sounds awful," I told my best friend. "I'm so sorry." Both of these things I said were lies. What Suzanne described didn't sound remotely "awful," and I didn't have any sympathy because I considered it all her own fault.

On the drive up she'd complained that her son never did anything for himself. Not laundry or lunches or even signing up for Accepted Students Day at the college he wanted to go to—Suzanne had to do it.

"How old is he now?" I asked. I knew the answer, but any other response might give away how I really felt. I'd parked and we had a few minutes before we had to go in.

"Eighteen." Suzanne sighed. "I know. He should be the one." But she didn't sound convinced.

My daughter, who's a year younger than Suzanne's son, takes care of just about everything for herself. If she doesn't sign up for things, she doesn't do them. My husband insists on it. Sometimes I'm not so sure it wouldn't be better to give her a little help, but Drew says she won't learn to stand on her own two feet that way. We have to think long-term, he says. What kind of grown-up do we want her to be?

Well, but she's only seven, I said. Then eleven, twelve, and fourteen. Even now, it doesn't seem unreasonable to offer a hand or at least some advice about the decisions she has to make, like what colleges to look at or whether it's worth it to stay in an after-school job as a cashier at a convenience store where the manager routinely shows off to his teenage employees his talent for catching flies in his bare hands and then peeling off their wings.

But I didn't want to be one of those parents who only give lip service to the idea of raising independent kids. And when Drew and I argued if, for example, I wanted to give Ella a ride somewhere when she could easily get there on her bike, it usually ended with me giving in. "I know," I'd say to him. "'What kind of grown-up.'" I just had to hope he was right—I was counting on it.

And *was* Suzanne my best friend? Sad to say, but I think so. Sad because we really only ever saw each other at our tennis matches. But when I had the stress fracture that time, she dropped off casseroles and called every day just to chat. She told me she'd been laid up once and remembered how long the days could be. I suppose if I ever needed someone in an emergency and my husband wasn't around, I'd call Suzanne. So yes, I guess I'd say best friends.

The match would start in ten minutes. We got out of the car, went into the club, and headed to the locker room to change. Our opponents, whom we'd already played once earlier in the season, huddled and spoke in mumbles. "Going over their game plan," I whispered to Suzanne. I meant it as a kind of joke, mocking not only those two women but also Suzanne and me, because what was this, Wimbledon, or only a weekday women's tennis league? From all the drama you saw on the court sometimes, you might guess Wimbledon. Ridiculous. I knew better and I tried not to, but sometimes I couldn't help getting caught up in it myself.

Suzanne smiled, then said, "Yeah, how should we play them? The tall one gets everything at the net. But the other one has all that slice." The last time we'd beaten these two, but only barely, so it could go either way.

We were the only undefeated team in the league, and the others were gunning for us. Or *were* they? Hard to tell. We all tried to give the impression that we were just out to have a good time—get some exercise and socialize before returning home to meet our kids after school—but who did we think we were kidding? It was more than that.

We went out with our opponents and began to hit. The feeling on the court was friendly enough while we were warming up. But as soon as the match started, it went downhill. We had two disputes in the first three games, both on line calls I made. I admit I wasn't sure about either of them, but if they were mistakes, they were honest ones. I suppose I could have corrected myself, but if you do that once, they feel free to question you every time. And what difference does one or two points make? It all comes out in the wash.

After the first call, our opponents just looked at each other, in a conspicuous way designed to make sure Suzanne and I noticed. The second time, they motioned us to meet them at the net. "Are we going to have problems again?" the tall one asked.

"There's no problem," I said. I looked at Suzanne to back me up, but she only gave us all a nervous smile. On the other side of the glass wall separating the viewing gallery from the courts, I heard their teammates clucking and laughing, which rattled me.

"Hey, thanks for the support," I told Suzanne under my breath, as we resumed our positions for the next game. I said it in such a tone that I knew she wouldn't miss the sarcasm.

"Leigh, those shots were good," she said, also quietly. "Can you just be a little more generous, when they're close?"

Well, this flustered me further, I probably don't have to say. It also made me feel all the more competitive, as if it was me against the three of them, instead of my partner and me as a team. Again we pulled out the win, and our opponents gave us limp handshakes at the net. Originally I'd planned to stay for the social part, the sandwiches and soft drinks the home team served when all the matches were done, but I told Suzanne I'd forgotten I had an appointment and needed to get back. She nodded, and it was obvious she didn't want to stay and chat with anyone, either.

Getting into the car for the drive home, I didn't feel the high I usually did after winning a match. We rode mostly in silence, and just before I turned onto her street Suzanne said, "Leigh, I hope you don't mind my saying this, but I think you might be getting a reputation. I've heard some talk about your calls, and not just today. I'm telling you this because I'd want to know, if it was me."

"Oh, for God's sake," I said. "'Some talk'? What does that mean?" Which was a dumb question, I admit. I knew very well what she meant.

But I had to throw something back at her, the way my grandfather told me they used to toss flak up to neutralize bombs launched from the sky.

Suzanne must have realized there was no need to answer. When we got to her house, she suggested we put this match behind us and look ahead to next week. I agreed, even though I intended to call our captain and resign from the team as soon as I got home.

"Oh, did you want to borrow that book?" Suzanne asked, as she pulled her bag out of the back seat. "I can run in and grab it."

There was a new book I kept overhearing people talk about, on the subject of parenting teenagers. Suzanne had told me it helped her a lot. "No thanks," I said, "I don't think I need it," and then I did my best to ignore the look she gave me and the sound she made, which I decided was just a friendly laugh.

When I got home my daughter was in the kitchen, chopping vegetables for soup. My tennis days were her days for providing dinner, because my husband hardly ever made it in time to eat with us, not that he would have cooked a meal—who am I kidding?—if he did. Ella asked how the match had gone, and I told her our opponents accused me of cheating. "That's awful," she said, squinting under the bill of her baseball cap at the carrot coins she'd just cut. She put the coins on top of each other, then spent a considerable amount of time slicing around the edges so all the pieces were the same size. "I'm sorry about that."

Something scratched at the back of my mind as I poured a glass of wine for myself: Why was she not more surprised at what I'd told her? But I erased it with the first sip.

"Did Mrs. Pinckney stand up for you at least?" Ella asked. I shook my head and told her I didn't think I was going to play in the league anymore.

My daughter burst out laughing. "Ha! That's a good solution, just quit when things get hard. I can only imagine if our situations were reversed right now, what you'd be saying to *me*."

"That's different," I said, though I felt trouble coming, like when you see police lights ahead.

"How?" She'd moved on to the celery, using her finger joints as a measuring guide. I watched and listened to the snip, snip of the knife until each piece looked the same, at which point she slid every one carefully into the pot.

"It just is. Honey, you know the veggies don't all have to be the same size, don't you? It doesn't matter. It's just soup."

"It matters to *me*," she said, and I was afraid to ask why. I was afraid it had something to do with the fact that she wore the baseball cap all the time now—not a team cap of any kind, just a plain gray one that went with everything, as much as a baseball cap can go with everything—even though Drew had asked her to keep it off in the house.

I topped off my glass. "Did you know Suzanne still makes Josh's lunch every morning? And signs him up for things, like info sessions and tours. All the stuff you've been doing for yourself for years."

"I heard he lost it," Ella said, though I wasn't sure I heard right because she spoke from behind the cupboard door as she reached for the soup bowls. "Is Dad going to be here, or is it just us?"

"Just us. Did you say he lost it? Who? Are you talking about Josh?"

"Who else? *Dad?*" The idea of her father losing anything—a button, a client, his mind—was laughable, given how much security and assurance he had built into his life. *Our* lives. That's what he was doing at the office right now: adding ramparts to the fortress and boulders to the dike.

"But what do you mean Josh lost it?" I asked.

"Freaked out. Went mental." She set down our spoons, then began adjusting them on the placemats, and I couldn't watch. "Not at school—on a weekend. Like, totally broke down. His mother had to bring him to the emergency room."

"When was *this?*" I was ashamed of the tone of fascination I heard in my voice, and hoped Ella hadn't detected it too. But what can I say? Fascination is what I felt, followed by sympathy for Suzanne and a measure of relief I couldn't ignore that it had been her kid instead of mine.

Ella shrugged. "I don't know. Like two months ago maybe." She turned her back to me more than she would have had to, merely to turn the knob on the stove. "I think he tried to kill himself."

Two months ago, our team season had been well underway. Suzanne and I would have already played at least four matches together. As partners. As friends—or at least, I thought so. Best friends! Yet she'd never once mentioned any trouble at home. Josh hadn't come up until earlier today, when she said he never did anything for himself.

"Was he acting weird before that?" I asked Ella, trying to keep my voice steady. "Were there any signs?"

"I don't think so. People said he seemed the same as always."

"So how is he now? And why didn't you tell me any of this before?"

She set our bowls on the counter. When Drew isn't here, we treat ourselves to eating in the kitchen. "I guess he's okay. I mean, he's back at school and everything. I figured she would have told you about it herself. You guys are friends, right?"

"Right," I said, though in the next moment I felt the same wave of guilt that comes with lying.

Poor Suzanne, I thought. Here she was dealing with all of this, and I'd given her a hard time for failing to stick up for me on a tennis court. I resolved to find a way to talk to her about it on the way to our next match. To apologize. I would be the bigger person. She'd thank me and say she was sorry she hadn't trusted me more, it was clear what a good friend I was. Just the prospect of having her tell me what she'd been through, and feeling closer to her, made me feel more cheerful as I approached the day.

It was her turn to drive to the match. When she picked me up she seemed in a good mood, and she didn't bring up the tension between us from the week before. I considered not mentioning what Ella had told me, but the conversation I imagined between us was so clear—and so rewarding—that I didn't resist. "Listen," I said, after we'd told each other we were fine, "Ella told me what happened with Josh a while ago. I'm so sorry, Suze."

I'd never called her *Suze* before. I wasn't looking at her as I spoke, so I don't know if her face reacted to this or to the sympathy I was trying to express. "Oh," she murmured over the steering wheel. "I just assumed you already knew. I thought everyone knew. I wondered why you never said anything."

"No! I didn't." Okay, so this gave me important information, and I was glad I'd brought it up. "She only told me the other day." When she just kept driving with her eyes straight ahead, I went on. "That must have been so scary."

"It was." She seemed to have more trouble getting those simple words out than she should have.

"I mean, I can't imagine."

She grew quiet. "You can't imagine because Ella would never do a thing like that, right?" She was smiling a little (I saw when I turned to look), as if she'd just won a secret bet she'd made with herself.

"No! That's not what I meant. I—"

Did I have what it took to bring up the uniform soup vegetables, the perfectly lettered flash cards, the requirements Ella had devised about the color of underwear she was allowed to wear on a given day? What would it take for me to confide in Suzanne about the clumps of hair I found every morning, pressed inside crumpled tissues in my daughter's bathroom?

Whatever it would have taken, I guessed I didn't have. But I closed my eyes and opened my mouth, preparing to fly blind into the heart of it—something I never do. I didn't get the chance, though, because Suzanne cut me off. "Never mind. Let's just get through the match, okay?"

I felt bad that she said *get through,* as if it were an obligation she'd be glad to have done with. I knew the right thing to do was shut up and agree. But my pulse was racing from the leap I'd almost made, and I couldn't resist adding, "Can I just say one more thing? I wasn't trying to upset you, I promise. I was trying to bring us closer, not further apart."

We'd pulled into our destination. Around us women wearing tennis backpacks bobbed toward the building. Suzanne turned the car off and slumped back in her seat. "Do you really care?" she asked. "About what happened with Josh? Or are you just… I don't know, fascinated?"

"Of course I care!" I said. "'Fascinated'? Of course I'm not *fascinated.* Why would you ask me a question like that?" Too late, I remembered my resolution to be the bigger person. Instead I'd just accused my friend and partner of accusing *me*.

"Never mind," she said again, getting out of the car. "Let's just drop it. Look, we're going to bend over backwards on the line calls today, right?"

If she hadn't said "we," I probably would have been able to say I was sorry about the conflict of the week before, and promise to be extra careful about how I saw the shots. But as it was I felt condescended to, because no one had ever questioned the way *she* called the ball. So I'm sorry to say I only made some noise I figured she could interpret however she wanted, and followed her into the club.

All was fine through most of the match, which was another close one. We won the first set but lost the second, then traded games in the third until our assigned time was almost up. With a few minutes left and the outcome in the balance, one of the women on the other side of the net hit an overhead at my feet. It was a crucial point, and that was what I focused on instead of where the ball landed.

I called "Out!" and shot a triumphant glance at Suzanne, because this just about clinched our win.

But Suzanne was looking elsewhere. Immediately the overhead hitter said, "No, no, no," and approached the net shaking her head. "You can't do that."

To be honest, I doubted myself, as I had in the match before. The right thing to do, the only thing to do, was apologize and say *You're right, I'm not sure, it's your point*. But it would have been another person, an alternate version of myself, who did this. What *I* did was stand firm in insisting, even when Suzanne suggested that as a middle ground, we could replay the point.

The team across the net didn't accept this offer. From the viewing area on the other side of the glass, I heard some boos. "I'm sorry," I said, and for a moment our opponents' faces softened as they waited for me to give in. "I know it looked close. But that ball was out."

Well, they ended the match then and there, even though we had some time left and theoretically, they could have caught up and eked out a tie. But they just shook their heads and gave snarky laughs, packed up their stuff and walked off the court without looking at either of us, let alone shaking our hands. "Oh, Leigh," Suzanne said. Through the glass, their teammates glared at us. "That was awful."

I hoped she couldn't tell how my fingers twitched as I returned my racket back to my bag. We hustled out of the club without going back to the locker room, which would have required walking past our now hostile hosts.

When we were halfway home I murmured, "I was afraid I would lose." It wasn't what I intended to say. I'd planned different words. But *I was afraid I would lose* is what came out.

Suzanne didn't respond, and I hoped I'd spoken too softly for her to hear. But then she said, "It's just a tennis match."

"I know," I told her. But this was a lie, too.

After she dropped me off, I went straight to my computer and sent an email to our team captain, copying Suzanne and saying I'd injured something during the match and would have to pull out for the rest of the season. I waited for Suzanne to call and try to talk me out of it, but the call never came. From my captain I received a terse note back: *Feel better*, followed by a smile emoji. That night, to distract us all from the routine argument about whether baseball caps should be allowed at the dinner table, I told Drew and Ella what had happened.

"Well, there goes your perfect record," Ella said.

"Actually," I told her, "a default still counts as a win."

My daughter laughed. Drew asked if I planned to take up another hobby.

"Hobby?" I asked. A hobby is not what tennis had been to me.

"You could try something you've never done before. Drawing. Quilting. I don't know, take a class just for the fun of it."

I almost laughed. As if *he'd* ever take a class for the fun of it, or try something he didn't already know he could do.

When spring came, the league ended and people began playing outdoors again. I saw them on the courts at the park every time I drove by. One day, Suzanne called; I saw who it was and hovered my hand over the phone for a moment, but didn't pick up. She left a message asking if I might want to go out and hit sometime, just the two of us. In her voice I heard forgiveness and invitation, and it filled me with joy. Is that too dramatic—an exaggeration? I'm tempted to call it that, but no. I'd had a hard few months, and it was joy I felt when I heard my best friend's voice and pictured us out on the court together, just playing for fun. Not caring where the ball went, meeting at the side of the court every so often to chat and turn our faces toward the sun.

And it *was* like that, at first. A glorious Saturday morning—the perfect temperature and no breeze. We hit with an old rhythm I'd forgotten, and it gave me even more pleasure than I'd imagined. After fifteen minutes I called her up to the net and asked if she wanted to play some points.

Her face fell. "Not really," she said. "I mean, this is nice, isn't it?" She gestured at the court where we'd been hitting the ball *to*, not away from, each other.

I shrugged. "Sure. Okay. It's all right."

She could have just smiled and started another rally. But—and this is why she's my best friend—instead she bounced the ball a few times, seeming to deliberate, then said, "I suppose we could play a few games."

She tapped the ball over the net and said I could serve first. I won that game and then the next two, and I felt lighter and happier than I had in a long time as we met at the side of the court for a water break. I told her, "I'm so glad you called and suggested this."

"Well, this isn't what I suggested, but never mind." She gave a weak wave, though I couldn't be sure at what.

"You aren't having fun?"

She looked at me sadly. "Yeah, it's fun," she said.

"Want to finish the set?" I started bouncing a ball to show I was eager to get back out there. Suzanne said *Sure* in a resigned tone, took a few steps onto the court, then turned and appeared to be in some kind of pain as she added, "You know, Leigh, it doesn't have to be this way. *You* don't have to be."

I caught the ball and looked at her, on the verge of asking what she meant. But I already knew. Besides, if I asked, she'd say it, and I didn't want her to.

What I wanted, so much, was to believe she was right. But I didn't dare, because what if she wasn't? My daughter had plucked herself almost bald by then, and it would have cost too much to find out.

The Forest

I said to my kids, "Trust me, you don't want to know. You'll wish you could go back to *not* knowing, but by then it'll be too late."

They do trust me—about everything. They're still that young. They'd believe me if I told them it's not true we all have to die someday, or that their father loves them very much. I don't like having all that power, and I'd give it back if I could.

My son told a joke last night at supper. I knew he didn't get it—it was just something he'd heard at school. It was a horrible joke, and I'm sorry to say I found it funny. "A boy and a clown walk into a forest. The boy looks around and says, 'Gee, this is kinda scary,' and the clown says 'How do you think *I* feel? I have to walk out of here alone!'"

I'm sorry to say I made the mistake of smiling. My sister laughed outright. "That's the worst joke I ever heard," she said, pointing her knife at Toby. "Also the best."

"What?" my daughter cried, lately desperate to learn the secrets of women. "Why is that funny? Who's the boy?"

Toby was so pleased with himself he almost levitated out of his chair. Making his aunt laugh is his highest glory.

My husband smiled at me from across the table. Well, no, he didn't, because he wasn't there—I've never had a husband, but if I *had*, that's where he would have been sitting and what he would have done. I need to stop saying *My husband this, my husband that*. It's never out loud, just in my head, but even so, it's a bad habit. Why waste time wishing?

But—just one more and then I'll stop—if I *had* a husband and he was sitting there, he would have said to me, "See what great kids we've raised? So sweet and so good? They have no idea what the world will do to them." That's when I shut him up and said to the kids, "Trust me, you don't want to know." They're sweet and good even without a father. Either I did something right or I just got lucky; I don't care which, as long as it lasts a little longer.

The movie we chose after supper was *Airplane!* We sat the way we always did, the four of us on the couch with our feet on the coffee table, one blanket covering us all. "Surely you know how bad your feet stink," Fiona would say to Toby, and he'd say, "Don't call me Shirley!" They know every line of the dialogue, and they crack up every time.

Next to me, my sister put her head on my shoulder. She stays with us whenever she comes for her treatments, because we live closer to the hospital than she does. When we first told the kids about this arrangement, Fiona froze at the word but Toby asked, "Hospital? What is it?" My sister immediately picked up her cue and said, "It's a big building with patients, but that's not important right now." They both cracked up and Carolyn went on to tell him, "Promise me you'll watch that movie every year on my birthday," and Toby shrugged and said, "Okay. You can watch with us."

Eight months ago I sat next to her, across from the doctor, when he explained that these injections—part of a clinical trial—were her best shot at survival. Until that appointment, we hadn't understood that she might not survive. Carolyn smiled. I saw that the doctor interpreted this as an inappropriate response to what he'd just told us, but *I* knew she believed he'd made a pun to lighten the mood (the injections were her *best shot*) and wanted to reward him for the effort.

That might sound nuts, but remember, we are women and he was a man, in a white coat to boot.

I've always been able to read my sister like this. Same for her with me. We're each other's emergency contact and next of kin. There hasn't been an emergency yet, but we're both ready.

"What if this is it?" she said to me the other day, when the kids were outside playing kickball with the triplets from down the street. "If this is it, what's the point? What's *been* the point? I mean really, Lex. I worked so hard for it all to pay off someday, but what if 'someday' doesn't come?" She'd worked herself into a state. Snot, tears, shouts—the whole nine yards. "I would have taken *so* many more days off. I would have spent all my money. Goddammit!"

It took her time to calm down, while I just sat with her. I knew I'd feel the same way if it was me, so I didn't try to talk her out of it. After a while she blew her nose and said, "It's just— I don't want to leave. I want to find out what happens."

She said this like a kid who wasn't being allowed to stay up to watch the next episode of her favorite show. Which I guess, in a way, she was.

"You can't think like that," I told her, breaking my resolution to let her feel whatever she wanted. "Try to expect the shots to work. That's what I'm doing."

"If this is it, though," she wailed (it was the first time I think I ever heard somebody actually *wailing* in real life), "it still means something, right? To you, at least. And the kids. *I* meant something. It will have mattered that I was here."

It was a question, but she said it like she was announcing a fact. *It will have mattered that I was here.*

"You moron," I said. This was how we'd been speaking to each other since we were kids. I didn't have to say anything else—she understood my answer.

AT WORK TODAY I TOLD THE JOKE TO PEOPLE in the break room. I got some groans and some clucks, but my friend Rafe liked it. "I mean it's gruesome, but not in a detailed way," he said, cracking pistachios into the Bills cap he always turns over on the table to collect the shells. "The humor's more nuanced. It catches up to you."

Rafe had a year of college, so words like "nuanced" come naturally to him. When he first got hired I thought there might be something between us, but when I asked him out for a beer after work one day, he told me he played for the other team. That's how he said it: "I hope it isn't too soon to mention this, Lexie, but I play for the other team." He leaned across the table and made sure I looked in his eyes. I admit I was embarrassed, and also a little pissed. Not at him, but nature. How many guys am I going to meet at that plant, in this town, who'd make a good husband and father?

Estelle, the only person who's been here longer than I have, patted her chest when she heard the punchline. She always tries to get out of doing things she's supposed to do by saying she has a heart condition. More than once I've told her, "Estelle, *everyone* has a heart condition," but she just ignores me and then I feel guilty for being mean and I end up doing the thing she got out of doing. When she acted as if my joke was about to give her a coronary, I apologized and offered to clean her machine when our shifts were over.

I didn't really mind because it made the end of the day come faster. Rafe and I punched out together, and he wished me luck. When I asked what for, he said, "She gets those tests back today, right? Your sister."

Well, no way would it do to let him know I'd forgotten. Is *forgotten* the right word? No it is not. But whatever the right word is, he put it back in my mind again. I thanked him and said for about the thousandth time, "You couldn't just *sub* for my team?", and we both gave tired laughs, but when I got out to my car I had to take a few minutes to cry into the steering wheel so hard I thought I might puke.

But luckily I had to pull it together, to go pick the kids up from school. How many times since Fiona was born have I thought this—how lucky I am to have these creatures I need to pull it together for? It wakes me up sometimes at night, how much I love them and (I know I'm not supposed to say this) how much I dread them growing up.

Fiona came out of the building first, her backpack bulging because it was library day and she can never choose just one or two books the way they're supposed to. Lately she's been on a Helen Keller kick. Sometimes I'll be walking by and she'll grab up my hand and start finger-spelling into my palm. "You know I don't get what you're saying, right?" I always tell her, and she shrugs and says it doesn't matter, she's just practicing.

She got into the car and said, "I think I know what happens in that joke" before she'd even buckled herself in.

"You do?" My heart clutched a little.

"The clown has to walk out alone because he's gonna leave the boy behind, right?"

"Yeah, I think so." I hoped to give the impression that I wasn't sure, myself.

"But why does he do that?"

I try to be honest with them, I do. But it was too soon for this one. Too soon. "Maybe to test him," I said, as Toby pitched himself into the car. "A challenge or something. To see if he can find his way home without any help."

"Oh, like Outward Bound." Her forehead unwound from its frown. She knew about Outward Bound because a kid I used a few times as a babysitter went through it. I'd told Fiona and Toby that Dylan had gone off to a program that would teach him about survival in the wilderness. I didn't tell them the program was court-ordered after he set fire to Chipotle when they wouldn't give him a raise.

They'd liked Dylan because the three of them made pizzas together and he let them put on whatever toppings they wanted, like popcorn and marshmallows. He started a tradition in our house, which we follow once a week now. The challenge is to think up the weirdest possible combinations but still produce pizzas people will eat. Sometimes it's a mistake to come to our table hungry on Thursday nights, but on the other hand it's always more fun than when I pick up something on the way home to stick in the microwave.

Tonight Fiona chose Doritos as her topping, and Toby picked bananas. I hadn't given it any thought, so at the last minute I pulled out the leftover Halloween candy and chopped up a few Snickers bars. That *really* made them happy and they ate every bit of it, caramel and all.

Carolyn didn't make it back from her appointment before we sat down to supper. I was both dying to know and afraid to hear what the doctor had said. Was it a good sign or a bad one that she hadn't texted?

At seven, she still hadn't arrived. I felt exhausted, and I wanted to get the kids to sleep so my sister and I could talk about whatever news she'd gotten, as soon as she came home. I told Fiona she could read either the first chapter of every book she'd brought home or five chapters of just one. She chose option two and settled into bed with *The Miracle Worker*, which she'd renewed for the third time. Toby was in one of his dawdling moods, so I said if he put on his pajamas and got into bed in the next ten minutes, I'd tell him a story. I had no idea what story I'd tell. And just before I would have had to figure it out, the back door banged open and Carolyn let out a giant, crazy holler that rang through the whole house.

It could only have meant one thing. I couldn't believe it. Even the doctor had told us not to get our hopes up, yet here was my sister hollering what I could tell was a hallelujah.

I closed my eyes and tried to keep the tears inside as Fiona came running. "What?" she cried to her aunt. "What happened?"

Carolyn lifted her higher than I would have thought she had the strength for. "Good news!" But we hadn't told the kids exactly everything, so she couldn't really go into detail the way she would with me later. Instead she said, "I got promoted," and I was impressed she'd thought of this because I guess, in a way, she had.

My sister must have seen that I was in no shape to tell a story, so she offered. All four of us sprawled across Toby's bed. "A boy and a clown walk into a forest," she began.

"Not the *joke*," Toby said, sitting up to object.

"Ssh. Lie down. It isn't the joke." Carolyn reached out to cup his chin, the trick we'd learned when he was a baby to settle him down. "A boy and a clown walk into a forest. The boy looks around and says 'Gee, this is kinda scary' and the clown puts a hand under his chin and says, 'I know. Here. Give me a minute.'"

I could tell from the way Toby's eyes darted how vivid the scene was to him. He breaks my heart at least once a day. Since Christmas, I keep flashing on his rendition of *The Messiah* from when we went to the sing-along at Rafe's church: "And we shall live for ever and eh-eh-ver!" He looked so happy, shouting up at the sanctuary ceiling, that I couldn't bear to correct him on the words.

"The clown points to a flat, smooth rock at the edge of the clearing," my sister went on, "a rock just big enough for the boy, and the boy goes over and sits. The clown takes off his backpack and starts rummaging around in it, then pulls out a pack of Wet Ones. He starts wiping the makeup off his face while the boy watches. It takes a pretty long time and the whole pack of cloths, but when he's done, he's gotten rid of every single trace of the white cheeks and the black eyes and the giant red smile. They're just a boy and a man now, having a talk in the woods."

A pause as Toby adjusted the image in his mind from *clown* to *man*. "What do they talk about?" he asked.

Carolyn shrugged. "Whatever the boy wants."

Toby considered. "I like that story," he said, and Fiona said she did, too.

"Is the man his father?"

It hadn't occurred to me that Toby might wonder that, but when he asked it, I thought, Duh! Of course. "I guess he could be," my sister said.

Fiona declared, "That story is *like* the joke, only better." She grabbed up my hand, and I waited for her to finger-spell something into it. But no, I guess she just wanted to hold on.

"I agree," Carolyn said.

"Because the other one... the *joke*..."

My sister waited a moment before she prompted, "The joke what?"

Fiona gave the big sigh that meant she'd bitten off more than her mind could chew. "I don't know. The punchline just kind of trails off."

I felt a whoosh rise up inside me, as if we were all speeding through an impossibly fun ride. I smiled and kissed both my kids on their foreheads. Toby smeared his off with the back of his hand before asking, "Is a forest the same thing as the woods?"

"I'm not sure. Why?"

He shrugged. "I don't mind woods. But I'm never going into a forest."

"Yes you are." His sister pointed—not at his face, but at his heart. "If you don't want to be a scaredy cat the rest of your life."

I waited for Toby to protest. But he was getting older. He was starting to understand there were things he would have to learn.

The four of us squished close to lie in a row. Looking up at the ceiling, I told them I thought the nearest forest was still pretty far away, but when it came time we'd all make the trip to it together.

The Daughter's Story

My name is Jen. and I'm an alcoholic. That's what I'm supposed to say when it's my turn in the circle, so I say it. But I feel like one of these days I'm not going to be able to hold it in anymore and I'll say what I'm really thinking, starting with *My name is Jen, and I killed someone.*

For the past fifteen months and four days I've made myself get up most weekday mornings when I'm basically still asleep and go to the Early Risers meeting in the basement of St. John's, where my parents got married and my brothers and I were baptized. I went to Sunday School in this basement and made my First Communion in the sanctuary upstairs, right before my mother moved away with my brothers and me. I tried to pay attention, but Sunday School was boring, and I both dreaded going and hated it when I was there. I wanted to be outside, running or riding, not stuck in the basement of some church.

The only time I ever went to confession was before my First Communion. I got through it as fast as I could—"Bless Me Father for I have sinned, I bit my brother and stole gum from my mother's purse, for these and all my sins I am truly sorry" (even though I wasn't)—and I didn't stick around long enough to hear my slate had been washed clean. I didn't care, because what does forgiveness mean to a first-grader?

Father Paul was assigned to the parish after my parents' wedding but before my oldest brother Cal was born, which means he and my father were best friends for more than twenty-five years. Even though he isn't a drunk himself, Father Paul comes down sometimes to stand at the edge of the meeting and listen. Nobody minds. It's an open meeting, anyone can come. He told me it inspires him to hear the things people say around that circle. How much they struggle but don't want to give in. Or, if they gave in yesterday, how hard they'll work not to give in today. He likes the slogans hanging on banners around the hall: *First Things First. Progress, Not Perfection. Let Go and Let God.*

Most days he joins us in taking hands to say the Lord's Prayer, then comes over to give me a hug before heading back up to the sanctuary. I felt self-conscious about the hug at first, till I realized everyone understood. This is a small town, and Father Paul and my father have been friends all these years. They're like brothers—or, at least, they were. Father Paul was like an uncle to my brothers and me: pulling pennies from behind our ears, making balloon animals at our birthday parties, that kind of thing. He came over for dinner every Wednesday, a ritual he and my father continued after the family broke up. I know how much my father needed both him and God, after the divorce. It's probably not a stretch to say Father Paul saved him.

My brothers and I used to make fun of our father for going to church every day. Now I'm the one in a church every day, and my father hardly ever goes.

Father Paul calls me Jennifer because my father does. I'm sure he thinks I like it, because I haven't corrected him. Why should I hurt an old man's feelings?

I'd give anything to be able to tell him the truth, which is that I only go by *Jen* now because it's my way of separating myself from the person who killed someone that night. Sometimes I imagine the look I'd see on his face if I confessed to him, and it brings me a moment of relief even though I'm only imagining the scene and what would follow: a trip to the police station to make it official. To own up to my crime. And if I was lucky, finally feeling better because I'd puked the poison out.

But I never allow this fantasy to last long. Since I'm not the only one I'd be turning in, it's not my right to confess.

"Haven't seen your dad in a while," Father Paul says this morning, when I step back from the hug. "He okay?"

"Sure," I say. "He's fine. Well, I mean, you know." We both understand that "fine" is relative when it comes to my father now.

"Do you think he'd want me to bring Communion to the house?" It's obvious he wants me to say yes. He's looking for an excuse to see his best friend, whether on church business or not.

He doesn't need me to answer. My father's faith is old-school. Receiving the Eucharist, he doesn't like to be *served*, like the Presbyterians who just sit in their pews and wait for the bread and grape juice to be brought to them. When he took Communion in the hospital after his legs got crushed, he insisted on getting out of bed to stand for those few seconds, with me supporting him on one side and a nurse on the other.

"It's just harder for him now," I tell Father Paul. "Walking. *Everything.*" On impulse I add, "It doesn't mean he doesn't love you anymore."

A mistake. I see the flash of hurt in the priest's eyes before he tries to hide it. "And how are *you?*" he asks. "When are you going to tell him where you really go every morning?" When I don't respond he touches my arm and says, "Jennifer. The truth requires a sacrifice sometimes."

What? But nothing in his face tells me he's offering advice more specific than any he'd offer his other parishioners.

I'm sure he thinks he's being profound. I'm sure he hopes his words will move me to take the action he thinks I should. But all I hear is another slogan, and if I hear another slogan, I just might scream.

"Soon," is the only answer I give him. I feel bad about how it comes out, but as much as I love him it's none of Father Paul's business what I tell my father, or when.

AND THE QUESTION ISN'T *when* I'm going to tell my father I go to meetings. What Father Paul really wonders is why I haven't done it already. It wouldn't exactly do to say I'm not sure I believe I'm an alcoholic. Yeah, I drank a lot after I killed someone. I went off the rails. But who wouldn't? Wouldn't you?

If I don't tell my father, I'm reserving the option of picking up again. Telling him would mean it's true. When I leave the house in the morning to head to Early Risers, I say I'm on my way to the gym.

For now, I'm giving the wagon a try because I'm not ready to give up yet. When I'm ready to give up, it'll be easy, I know what to do. I was already doing it before I moved back here.

There's this old-timer at the meeting everyone calls Carrie Nation, because she flat-out admits she hates booze so much she'd walk into bars and smash all the bottles with a hatchet if she could get away with it. Carrie likes to say "Don't give up five minutes before the miracle," and I admit it blew my mind the first time I heard it. I mean who'd dare raise up the glass if they thought they risked blowing an actual *miracle* headed their way, in less time than it takes for our oldest horse Sammie to walk around the ring?

Nobody's bringing Patrick Mitchell back, and I can't find a way out of what I'm stuck in. Those are the miracles I'd choose, if I could.

But I guess the point is, you don't summon a miracle. A miracle appears.

This morning after the Lord's Prayer a few of the Early Risers invite me to go to Dunks with them, the way they do every day, but I tell them I have to work. This is a lie, I could make the time, but I know the next thing they'll be pushing on me is to get a sponsor, and I know what having a sponsor means. It means you have to tell the whole truth. So no, no sponsor for me.

In the parking lot I hear Griff Hackett behind me calling "Hey, Jen, hold up." I think about pretending I don't hear him, but how childish is that. "We meeting up later?" he asks, when I turn around and try to put on the smile I know he wants to see.

He smells good. If I asked him to, he'd tuck me against his chest. He's six-three, eight inches taller than me, and I could hide in the tent his arms make. Sometimes I do.

He'd keep me there as long as I wanted. Well, until he had to go to work. And he wouldn't ask why.

I recognized Griff my first time at the meeting. He was in my brother Cal's class, five years ahead of me. In seventh grade they got in trouble together for getting stoned one Saturday night, then stealing an ice-cream truck and destroying the football field by zigzagging from one end zone to the other. When he introduces himself in the circle he says "I'm Griff and I turned my life around," instead of the usual line. Maybe he thinks he's not really an alcoholic either? Or maybe he just likes doing things his own way.

"Sorry, I can't," I tell him, and I know he won't ask *why* about this, either. "But see you in the morning, right?" It's the way we all say goodbye after the meeting—by promising we'll show up for each other the next day.

Griff says "Sure," and if he's disappointed, which I know he must be, it doesn't show. He hesitates, then asks if I'm okay. I tell him yes, even though "okay" is relative when it comes to me now. He gets in his Silverado and salutes on his way out of the lot.

Only then do I realize that Carrie Nation's been standing behind us smoking, close enough to hear everything Griff and I said to each other. After he leaves, she flicks ash and tells me, "You're only as sick as your secrets, chicken."

Another slogan. It's either scream or laugh. I choose laugh, but I can tell I don't fool Carrie.

It's April, every day warmer and lighter, the saving grace of living in New England. You see your big jacket in the closet and think, Maybe I'm done with that for the year! (You're usually wrong, but it's still a nice feeling.) Two days ago it hit eighty and everybody had shorts on, but now it's back to normal, a sweatshirt in the morning and short sleeves by lunch.

It's going to be a beautiful day. It's a beautiful day already, and it fills me with dread. Until two years ago, I loved coming to the end of the school year in Florida (so hot, so boring) and looked forward to visiting my father in Massachusetts for his six weeks of custody beginning with the Fourth of July. It was me and my three brothers for those first years after the divorce, and then one by one the boys aged out and moved on. Four years ago, after my high school graduation, it was just my father and me. We found new routines and rhythms with just the two of us, although a lot of times the house had other people in it, either Father Paul or the friends I'd kept since kindergarten, mainly Betsy and Liz. My father liked when my friends came over. He taught them how to ride, and he teased us about the way we'd shut up when he walked into the room now that we were young ladies, so different from the way it was when we were kids and he had to ask us to pipe down.

"Young ladies" made us all blush. I felt sorry for my father because Liz and Betsy thought he was being ironic, using such a throwback term, but I knew he meant it.

Summer hasn't been the same since I killed Patrick Mitchell and then understood that I didn't have the option of coming clean. Paying the price. Last year, the first one after the accident and the first I lived here full-time, I kept myself so busy with work—and with running on our trails after I was done at the stable—that I managed to distract myself, mostly, from recognizing how nice the days were. I didn't want to let myself be seduced by the warmth or the sun, the rewards people who live in New England wait for all year. I knew I didn't deserve them.

Do I have another summer like that in me? Even just thinking about it is exhausting. But that's where the slogans come in, right? *One Day at a Time.*

In the parking lot at St. John's, I take a few extra seconds to just stand there and listen to the birds. Beyond the church, taller than the steeple, there's a pine tree with a blotch at the trunk's bottom, where the bark's scraped off. It looks like a skinned knee, but it would take a lot more than that to injure such a big tree.

My brothers used to climb that pine when we were kids. Every June St. John's holds a strawberry festival, with long tables laid out on the lawn behind the church, and one time Cal hid in the tree's branches and dropped raisins on people as they came for their strawberry sundaes. It would have been a stupid but harmless prank, if one of the older parishioners hadn't freaked out and fallen trying to dodge what she felt dropping from above. Father Paul went easy on Cal, just asking him to apologize to Mrs. Klett, who took it well and tried to laugh at herself. But our parents grounded him. I remember Cal protesting "It was *raisins!*" and that became an in-joke among us kids, code for when you wanted to tell somebody they were making a bigger deal out of something than it needed to be.

I loved the strawberry festival. It was my favorite thing. We always got a warm and sunny day, and I remember from the year I was five or six sitting there with my sundae turning to soup and having the sudden and distinct feeling that we all loved each other—not only my parents and my brothers and me, but everyone gathered on that church lawn to laugh and eat and play. To celebrate. I remember thinking it had all been arranged by God, and that this was how he wanted our lives to be.

Is it too much to wish for, to have a moment like that again? Probably. But at least I know it's possible. I bet there are lots of people who never get that gift.

The birds are singing like crazy when I get in my car, a Ford Focus, which still feels new to me even though we bought it used. My father insisted on it when he got home from the rehab center and saw my old Hyundai in the driveway. I'd had enough sense to pick him up from rehab in his own truck, but I should have realized how shocked he'd be when we pulled up at home and he saw the Hyundai sitting there. "I know," I told him, "but I can't afford a new one." He made us drive to the Ford dealership that same day.

Cresting the hill (*that* hill, the one I always hold my breath on), I see orange in the sky ahead and feel a strange, sudden mix of elation and alarm. It surges in me as I register two thoughts almost at the same time: *The sun never looks like that* and *That is not the sun.*

Fire. The word comes to me a split second before I register what the orange is, and where it's coming from—before I understand it's at our stable. Gunning the gas, I try to convince myself I'm seeing wrong, it's just an illusion, but of course this doesn't work because it's not.

I RACE DOWN OUR LONG DRIVEWAY and into the stable's parking lot with a screech. Even before I jump out I've counted the number of horses I can see: all of them. I just about puke from relief. We keep fourteen, and they're following their morning routine, with three already brushed and tacked for our first riders of the day, the others in the pasture eating hay. Our barn manager Jerzy and his wife Bridget have tied the most skittish ones to the fencepost farthest from the fire, because we all know that a horse who panics might run back into a burning barn to the stall he knows as home.

Jerzy gives me a somber thumbs-up, his face almost as grave as it was after my father got hit. Turning, I see my father take it all in from as close as he can get while still staying safe from the fire. He's leaning on his cane harder than he should need to. As the engines screech in, he wobbles. It hurts me to watch.

I turn back to the barn, where the intense orange spits and blazes through the dormer roof above the hayloft, before spiraling into gray and black smoke obscuring the sun. It hasn't caught yet in the ground floor, and from my angle it looks for a moment, weirdly, as if that end of the barn is wearing a triangular orange hat.

I hadn't been wrong, when I first saw that vivid color in the sky ahead of me—it *is* beautiful. If we were all watching a bonfire someone had set on purpose, we'd have an entirely different set of feelings from the ones that consume us now, as the giant curl of flames consumes the roof above the loft. I hear it crackle, then roar and huff as it chases air to feed on.

Finally, our old mare Sammie starts to freak out. She rears and whinnies, which makes the other horses think about acting up. Just in time, Bridget turns her in the pasture so she can't see the fire. Sammie calms down. Another thumbs-up from Jerzy as men jump from the engines and start running toward the flames.

SAMMIE'S THE OLDEST HORSE WE HAD LEFT after I took over for my father and convinced him to partner with the therapy clinic on the other side of the river. After his accident last year, he couldn't manage the stable by himself, so I offered to stay. I had nothing to go back to in Florida, aside from officially flunking out of school and listening to my mother say she was worried about me.

It didn't start right away. Back in Kissimmee after killing Patrick Mitchell, for a few weeks I managed to feel the same relief I brought from Massachusetts, when I realized there was nobody following in my rearview because my father had fixed things for me.

But it was a false euphoria, the same one I'd felt in putting on an act for my friends after that night on the beach and before I left to go back to my mother's. I told myself it was a good thing, because all the energy I threw into seeming normal was energy I couldn't spend on remembering what I'd done.

When the relief wore off, like a layer of skin that had covered my guilt, I began buying nips of Dewar's by the dozens—easier to hide in a purse or a backpack. It would have been so much easier if my mother had figured out I was drunk all the time, and forced me to do something about it. Get help or move out.

But it would never have occurred to her that I could be drunk all the time, because I was a good girl. I kept telling myself *I have to stop, I have to stop.* But by the time we got the call about my father's accident, I couldn't stop.

He got sideswiped by an SUV on his way across the river for morning Mass. If he'd stuck to St. John's and Father Paul he wouldn't have had that far a trip, but I ruined Father Paul for him. After my mother and I got the call I drove up to Massachusetts in two long days, getting a late start on both of them because I was hungover. When I went back to the house after seeing my father in that hospital bed, I looked up meetings and found the Early Risers. I only planned to stay sober while I was living in the house and taking care of him. And it only worked, those first days, because I knew it was temporary.

I helped him through the worst of it, until he graduated from a walker to the cane. He'll probably never ride again—a loss he hasn't talked about yet, at least with me—and most days his balance is so iffy he's afraid to drive. Jerzy or I take him wherever he needs to go.

I've never asked my father, but it's hard to imagine he doesn't think, the way I'm tempted to, that getting hit by a car—on his way to Mass, no less—is a punishment for what we both did.

By the time he was better, I liked my life up here more than the one I'd left in Kissimmee, where I didn't have much going on aside from what I learned in the meeting rooms is called *wreckage*. In fact I always liked my life in Massachusetts, except for the day my mother drove my brothers and me away with the U-Haul when I was little, and the night Patrick Mitchell died. Hadn't I even thought about moving up here to finish school? So I asked my father if he wanted me to stay on, even though (or maybe because?) I knew it meant I wouldn't be able to drink the way I'd been drinking in Florida.

When my father was in charge of the stable, he kept thirty horses and gave lessons and trail rides. I trimmed the operation to make things more manageable, and I could tell this worried my father because it meant less money coming in. But what could he say? He'd had his lawyer draw up the papers. He'd signed the reins over to me.

I did my research while he was still in rehab and talked to people at the psychology clinic, and we launched an equine-assisted therapy business called Horse Sense. It's a perfect fit for us because the horses I kept are the older, quiet ones who're happy to just stroll around the ring carrying someone on their back. Most of our riders have a history of anxiety or trauma, or for some other reason find it easier to be with horses than humans. If you've ever spent time around a horse, I don't have to explain this to you. And if you haven't, you should try it sometime.

We work with some veterans and some kids with autism, but most of our clients come from an after-school program for at-risk adolescent girls. It's kind of amazing to watch their faces change—transform, really—after just a single session of brushing a horse or feeding it peppermints out of their palms.

After his early doubts, I can tell my father likes what the stable's become. We're doing better financially than we were before, and our mission suits his desire and what he considers his moral obligation to ease suffering where he can.

In rebranding his business as a way to heal people, was I looking for a way to rebrand and heal myself? Of course. Has it worked? Of course not. But it does work for our girls—or most of them, anyway.

AS SOON AS THE FIRE CHIEF, FRANK VITELLO, learns there's no one in the barn that needs rescuing and the horses are safe, he directs his men to focus on containing the flames to the hayloft. It's a volunteer crew but they know what they're doing, this is the country and they've been down this road before.

Then, in the instant before anyone understands what's causing it, there's a shift in the air. The relief we all felt at seeing the horses safe in the pasture turns to a disbelieving, collective fright as Sammie jerks her rope loose and storms toward the barn. Jerzy chases her and yells, but it's a fool's errand, she's made up her mind and gallops toward the stall Jerzy saved her from when he first saw the fire.

Next to me, it's pure instinct that makes my father start toward her, but he's forgotten he can't run anymore and he stumbles on gravel, breaking the fall by throwing out his hands. My own instinct sends me toward *him*, and when I crouch down my eye catches something glinting on the ground beside the barn wall—silver, a rectangle—and a second later, recognizing it, I pitch myself over to grab up the lighter and plunge it into my pocket. My father's already making his way to a stand, frustrated but not badly hurt, and he motions me into the barn where Jerzy, Bridget, and one of the firefighters are already trying to force Sammie back out of her stall.

Then another shock: it's Griff Hackett who's pulling at the rope they've looped around the horse. Recognizing him makes me stop short for a second, before Bridget yells "Let me push!" and runs behind Sammie, a dangerous move but the only one left to us. Bridget yanks off her sweatshirt and throws it over the mare's eyes. Instantly Sammie relaxes, settling down enough so that when Bridget gives her a heave from her hind, the four of us manage to shove her from the stall, past the burning hay bales and back out to the fresh air. The cover has fallen off her eyes and she starts rearing again, but then she pulls up short with a leg lift and we realize the noise is pain, not resistance—she's hurt her hoof.

"Goddammit," Jerzy breathes out like a prayer, patting Sammie. "Just a few more steps, sweetheart." He coaxes her over to the post and this time secures her so she can't get away. "Good girl. We got you." To Bridget he shouts, "Bucket of water! Cool, not cold," and Bridget runs a pail over to the spigot at the side of the house.

My father's made his way down to Sammie, hobbling more noticeably than before his fall. He let his cane drop somewhere along the way and his hands are bleeding, but he doesn't notice or doesn't care as he puts his face close to Sammie's and whispers. The sight almost undoes me, but his voice has always soothed her like nothing else can. She settles and sighs into his sleeve.

I never saw Griff come back out of the barn after we rescued Sammie, and for a moment my heart skips thinking he's still in there, but then I see him among the guys on the crew turning their hoses full-blast against the fire. My face feels singed from the heat and we all move farther away, coughing. Despite the high pressure of the streams, the whole barn goes up before us. My father makes a sound like he's being strangled. Well, in a way he is.

It's another hour before they turn off the hoses. Every time I move, the lighter I picked up bounces in the pocket against my thigh. Our vet arrives to check out Sammie, bandaging the injured hoof but also confirming the signs of colic we were already worried about even before she suffered the stress of the fire. Jerzy makes some calls and we find temporary stall space—horse people come together that way—and he and Bridget start the process of loading the first few into trailers to begin the series of trips it will require. My father and I divide our goodbyes among the horses, promising we'll come get them as soon as we can. He takes extra time with Sammie, who nips at his jacket as if to say *Don't make me go!* She's our nervous girl. But that's what makes her so good with other nervous girls.

Frank Vitello directs Griff and another crew member to start raking the debris with pike poles, checking for sparks or embers they may have missed.

"Any idea how it started?" my father asks Frank. His voice sounds thin, as if the fire stole air from his throat. The blood on his hands has dried and I notice a cut on his forehead. He looks as if somebody beat him up. Well, the fire has.

Frank shakes his head and says they haven't found anything. Now's the time to pull out the lighter and show it to them, but I don't. Frank says that all the rain we've had lately must have moistened the hay, and then the sudden heat made it combust. Griff comes over to report nothing's burning now. I say to my father, "Remember Griff? We go to the same gym," and Griff catches on and nods, his promise to me that he's not going to give up how we really know each other.

"I remember," my father says. "How you doing, Griff." It's not really a question, but it doesn't sound hostile, either. Some parents would have decided to believe their own kid wouldn't steal an ice-cream truck and ruin a football field unless some other kid put him up to it, but my father always had his eyes open when it came to my brother Cal.

Frank says they'll come back every few hours to check on things before declaring an all-clear. I walk Griff back to the engine parked on grass turned black by flames. "You never told me you were a fireman," I say, realizing too late that it sounds like an accusation. "I thought you worked at Ace."

"I do. Unless a call comes in. Then I do this." He gestures at the collapsed barn, the haze of smoke around us, and the charred ground beneath our feet.

IT WAS A STUPID APOCALYPSE MOVIE my friends and I went to see the night Patrick Mitchell died. But we didn't care how dumb the movie was because we'd smuggled in a couple of six-packs, which we popped open on the way to the theater. I knew better, but I didn't argue very hard because I only ever saw Liz and Betsy for the six weeks I came up here in the summer, and I wasn't about to spoil the fun. Besides, we'd always been good girls, so why shouldn't we be rewarded? We believed we were smart enough to keep ourselves safe.

After the movie we drove to the beach, where someone had left behind a pair of paddles but no ball. Liz and Betsy tried batting a dead snail between them, and then a shell, but of course, neither of these worked. "What we just did was something only very drunk people would do," Liz said, and this struck us all as extremely funny.

But it made me slow down on the beer. Not because I was driving, I'm ashamed to say, but because I could never stand lying in bed with what Liz called the spin-dizzies. Sprawled on the blanket, close enough to feel the ocean's spray, we shot the shit and smoked from the pack of Newports we'd bought along with the Bud. I never smoked in Florida, but I did up here. My father wasn't crazy about it, but he said he'd rather I didn't hide it from him. I took a cigarette and lit it behind the windscreen Liz made for me with her hair.

But after I inhaled too hard and began coughing, I stubbed it out in the sand.

"Lightweight," she scoffed, in a way that said she loved me, and I thought, I *do* have sisters. Here they are.

Both of them went to the public university half an hour south of us, but they never made me feel bad about only being in community college in Florida. They understood I was doing it part-time and kind of ad hoc because I wasn't sure what degree to go for. "Come up here when you get your associate's, and finish with us," Liz said. "Wouldn't it be cool if you lived here all the time and we didn't have to cram everything in?"

I said it was tempting, but my mother probably wouldn't go for that. Then again, the house in Kissimmee *was* getting a little crowded now that her fiancé had moved in. "Would your father ever get married again?" Liz asked, and I asked why, did she want to be my stepmother, and she said No, but maybe my step-*sister*—her mother had said a few things.

I couldn't tell if she was joking, like I was, but if she wasn't, I didn't want to hear any more. I said, "You know how Catholic my father is. He'll consider himself married until either he or my mother dies."

"Does that mean he doesn't have sex?" She said it with a straight face, but there was a smile in her voice.

"Jesus. Can we not?" I made a circle in the sand with my sneaker toe, so I'd have something to look at instead of her. "Why are we talking about my father's sex life instead of yours?"

Liz shrugged. "I just think religion is funny. You do something you know you're not supposed to, but then all you have to do is tell a priest you did it, and he's like, 'Okay, just say this prayer and you're good to go.'"

"That's not exactly the way it works." But I wasn't in a position to explain how it did work, so I shut up and looked at the waves.

Betsy said priests usually gave her the creeps, but she didn't feel like that when she was at our house with Father Paul. "Of course not," I said. "I've known him forever. He and my father go back to before I was born."

Liz asked what my father got out of it and I told them he and Father Paul talked a lot, about God and the right way to live. Liz groaned. "Shoot me now," she said, draining one beer and opening another.

I told them they did regular stuff too, like watch Red Sox games and go fishing. They used to hunt ducks, until I asked my father to stop and get rid of the gun. "Good job," Betsy said. "Because poor duckies." She and Liz found this hilarious, too.

Even if we were still in touch, I probably wouldn't bother telling them my father ended up trading one gun for another. After his accident he bought a pistol to keep in his nightstand, because he couldn't move like he used to and he wanted to be able to protect himself and me, if it came to it.

Liz offered me another cigarette and I said I'd better not, because my father didn't like smelling it on my hair when I got home. "He knows you're a grown-up, right?" she said, and I said of course he did.

"Anyway, think about it," Betsy said as we stood to shake the blanket out, and I said, "Think about what?" and she said, "Moving up here. Going to school."

I said I would. I said I liked the idea, and suddenly, I did. I *was* a grown-up. Why couldn't Florida be the place I visited, instead of Massachusetts? Maybe it was time to think about where and how I wanted to live, instead of just doing what my parents expected because I was the youngest. And the only girl.

It was a good feeling, imagining a fresh start and independence. I'm sure part of the enthusiasm I felt came from the beer, but that wasn't all of it. When we got to the car Liz asked if I wanted her to drive, since I'd been doing it all night, but I told her I was fine. She was still drunk, but I'd come at least halfway to my senses. The truth was that I didn't want anything interfering with the vision I'd conjured of myself, as a person who might have a life that surprised her, if she took the right steps now.

Leaving the beach I turned the music up, and Liz asked if we could stop for another six-pack to keep the buzz going. She cracked a new one open and offered me the bottle, but I shook my head. I drove Betsy home first, and when I pulled up in front of Liz's she left the beer in the cupholder between us. "Promise you'll apply!" she shrieked, pointing at me like a parent giving a kid an order, and I grinned as I pointed back and said maybe in the morning.

I left the window open to let in some air as I drove past Jake's, the dive we'd all gotten into as high schoolers with ridiculously mediocre fake IDs Betsy's brother made us for ten bucks apiece. I was alone on the road as I picked up speed on the hill, no other lights ahead or behind me, and my hair flew around in the breeze. I lifted the beer Liz left, then saw my future self again in my mind's eye, and put the bottle down. Right after I crested the hill, something moved in front of me. I swerved, then hit it. Whatever it was had crossed my lights, but I thought it was just my bangs blowing in front of my eyes.

But a moment later my brain caught up to the image of a person's body having been lit up in my beams. I looked ahead and off to the side, but didn't see anything in the road or in the ditch at the side. Is it possible for a living heart to freeze? Or for a brain to? After those seconds of paralysis I stomped on the gas, floored it all the way home, and knocked on my father's bedroom door to tell him I'd hit somebody with the car.

He tried not to let me see him panic, but of course I did. He asked me questions and I answered them. Maybe I was hysterical, because he poured me whiskey and told me to calm down. Then he said he was going out, I should sit tight, he'd be back.

I figured he'd gone to the police station, to tell Steve Hinchey what had happened—to grease the skids, sort of, before bringing me to turn myself in.

Alone at the table, I poured more whiskey and smoked Newports without feeling or tasting a thing. When my father came back he poured a drink for himself and told me that the person I'd hit—and yes it was a person, not a deer or a coyote as I'd sat there trying to convince myself—was dead.

"You sure?" I asked, and he nodded and said the guy probably died before he hit the ground. Then I asked, "Who was it?" and he said he didn't know.

When we went out to inspect the Hyundai, we found the fender and headlight smashed. My father shined a flashlight around the outside and then the inside of the car. He said we should get rid of the empties, and I pulled them all out.

I said I thought he'd gone to the police, and he didn't answer. Back inside, he told me to try to sleep. Only then did I realize how tired I was, and how drunk, and I lay there with the spin-dizzies until I passed out.

WHEN I GOT UP THE NEXT MORNING, it was raining and the sky was dark, but there were birds at the feeder outside the kitchen window. I let them hypnotize me as I waited for coffee to brew. It took me a while to realize I was alone in the house because my father's truck was still in the driveway, but then I saw that wherever he'd gone, he'd taken my Hyundai. This time I felt sure he must have gone to the police, to show them the damage to my car and maybe find out whatever he could about the person I'd hit. Prepare whoever was on duty for when I turned myself in. People respect my father in this town, and he might have believed this would make some difference in how I'd be treated. When he drove Cal in after his night of carousing and theft and vandalism with

Griff Hackett, the officer taking the report said he was sorry to have to do it, he'd done worse things himself when he was a kid but wasn't lucky enough to have a father who made him stand up and take responsibility.

I'm sure Cal wanted to roll his eyes at that but he wouldn't dare, with my father standing right there.

The wind from the night before had given way to a rainy day. From the kitchen window I watched Jerzy and Bridget lead the horses into the pasture for their morning exercise and fresh air. I took a shower and got dressed, assuming that my father would return any minute to pick me up for the drive to the public safety building.

I didn't eat anything, figuring I might puke from fear. What was about to happen to me? Jail, I knew. We had one in this town, but maybe they'd send me down to Boston. The only things I knew about jail came from movies and TV. Did I have that in me? How did *anyone* have it in them? And if I didn't have it in me, what then?

Would it happen right away? Would I get bail, and if so, could my father afford it? Did I want him to? There'd be a trial, right? Well, not if I pled guilty. How long before I'd be free?

And beating underneath all these, like a heart outside my body: who was it I'd hit?

I was still standing at the window when my father pulled in. I saw the damage to the front end of the Hyundai and thought, *Wait*. It looked far worse than what I remembered seeing in the trail of the flashlight the night before.

My father came in and told me he'd gone over to St. John's, intending to see Father Paul and receive Communion, but after turning into the parking lot he'd driven into the big pine tree at the side of the rectory.

"Wait," I said, "you're saying you had an accident? But that's too—"

Too coincidental, I would have said. But I didn't, because in that moment I realized it *was*.

My father said he'd blacked out a little, right before hitting the tree. Father Paul ran out and wanted him to see a doctor, but my father told him he was fine.

"Did you—" *Did you confess?* But I could tell my father didn't want me to finish the question. I got no further before he shook his head and told me he'd take the Hyundai to Guidry's for repairs, before I had to drive it back to Florida. Then he said he'd better help with the horses, because of the rain.

It took me longer than it should have to piece together what he'd done: re-damage my car, with his best friend the priest as a witness, so that when he took it into the shop, nobody would question how the front end got mangled.

It rained all that day. A couple of kids went out to play when it finally stopped, and found Patrick Mitchell off the side of the road. He was nineteen—a year younger than me—and he was an apprentice to a plumber. Nothing in the news report made me think he'd been alive for any time after I'd hit him. But nothing made me think he *couldn't* have been saved, either.

There was a week and a half left before I was scheduled to drive back to Florida. My father had the car fixed, and I still saw Liz and Betsy almost every day because that was our routine. That's when I pretended that nothing had happened, and my father did the same. They teased my father, saying it's the *kid* who's supposed to wreck the *parent's* car.

The day I left, my friends and I hugged goodbye the way we always did. Out of my father's hearing, they said to let them know when I'd arranged to transfer to their school. They'd take me out to celebrate and introduce me around.

Little did any of us know that when I ended up moving here five months later, it wouldn't be to enroll, but to take care of my injured father. At first I'm sure they figured that's why I didn't call them and didn't want to go out—because I was busy with him.

But when he got better, I still didn't call or respond to their messages, because seeing my friends and not being able to tell them what happened that night would be worse than not seeing them at all. Maybe Liz thinks I'm pissed because of the step-sister comment she made on the beach. Maybe Betsy thinks I consider her too immature. Whatever they've told themselves, they don't call anymore. When my father asks about them, I say it happens, we've just gone our separate ways.

AFTER THE FIRE I PUT DOWN SOME KIND of lunch for my father and me, but I'm sure neither of us will remember, in an hour, what it was. The house itself feels as dazed as we are. I keep catching myself looking out the window expecting to see what I usually see—Jerzy and Bridget, and a teenager or two currying horses or being led around the ring—and the sight of the scorched barn frame comes as a shock every time.

I need to tell my father about the lighter I found at the fire, but we have things to do first. We split up the calls to the insurance company, clients with upcoming sessions, the farrier, the hay supplier, and the contractor, so we can get started on a new barn right away. I can tell my father's anxious to finish his list so he can go back and check on Sammie. Bridget's with her, walking Sammie around because that's the best thing for colic, and the next few hours should tell us whether she'll live or die.

Jerzy pulls in and gives a quick beep. My father gets up from the table, but I ask him to wait a sec, I have to show him something. I see him brace at the words, and I don't blame him. From my pocket I pull out the Zippo and open my hand. One side of the lighter case is melted, but we can still make out the chrome scroll design and the monogram *KJM* on the other.

My father gasps. Even without the initials, we'd both know who the lighter belongs to.

Our guests aren't allowed to smoke on site, of course. Nobody is. But during one of her first therapy visits, as she waited for Sammie to be tacked up, Kelly Mitchell pulled out the Zippo and snapped it repeatedly into flame, before my father asked her in his quiet voice to stop. She flushed and said she was sorry. She told us she didn't smoke—I guessed she wanted my father to know that—but her uncle who gave her the lighter assumed she did, and it helped her nerves to flick it sometimes.

My father's never been a loud talker, but in our kitchen I have to strain more than usual to hear what he's saying when he asks where I found it. When I tell him outside the hayloft, he winces; maybe he was hoping it was an incidental discovery, farther removed from the fire. "Are we going to do something with this?" I set the lighter on the table. "Like show it to Frank?"

I know the answer before he shakes his head. He doesn't have to tell me we're not turning the lighter in, and he doesn't have to tell me why. We've done enough to Kelly and her family already.

Then he reaches for the Zippo, but I get to it faster and say, "That's okay, I'll take care of it."

He gives me a look I can't read. He's used to me wanting to lighten his workload, but this isn't a task he'd expect me to take when he already claimed it.

Then Jerzy beeps again, and we both know my father has to get back. He tells me to hold down the fort—"what's left of it," he says, making a grim joke—and I say I will.

After he leaves I sit perfectly still at the table, but my nerves are blazing. Did Kelly set the fire as revenge because she found out I killed her brother? What other reason could there be?

But how *could* she know?

Sometimes I open the cupboard to see if the whiskey bottle's still there. It always is, and sometimes I take it out and put it on the table. Sometimes I pull out the egg timer—which my mother didn't value enough to take with her, and which my father cherishes because she used it every day—place it next to the bottle, set it for five minutes, and wait. When nothing comes to me, or changes, I set it again.

I do that now, once my father's truck has pulled out. There's forty seconds left on the third five minutes when another truck pulls in, and I look out to see Griff Hackett's Silverado. I shove the bottle back in the cupboard, but he doesn't come to the door right away. Maybe he's not coming to the door at all; I watch him use the pike pole again to comb the ground where the barn stood, giving the rubble a once-over. I don't know whether it would be a good idea or a bad idea to call out to him.

But I don't have to decide, because once he finishes his inspection he approaches the house, looking as if he doesn't know whether to knock or not. "What took you so long?" I say from behind the screen, hoping he'll know I'm mocking myself after rejecting him this morning.

He grins. I wouldn't exactly call it a shit-eating one, but it's close. "I told Frank I'd come over and check for hot spots," he says, stepping toward me slowly as if he's still not sure I'll invite him in. "What do you think, Jen? You got any hot spots?" and from there it's about ten steps and fifteen seconds to my bed.

Half an hour later I'm lying inside his arms, waiting for him to fall asleep so I can start trying to figure things out, but he doesn't. We're both facing the window and the sun's about to set. Smoke still floats and settles in the air outside, making it look darker than it is. "You were a hero today," I tell him, and when he makes a *Yeah, right* sound I say, "No, really. You saved Sammie."

"He going to be okay?" Griff asks, and I tell him Sammie's a girl and we don't know yet, colic can kill a horse, but we've got our vet on the case. I pull Griff's hand up tight to my chest and feel the raised dark scar I've seen there before, but this time I ask how he got it. "You'll laugh," he says, and I promise not to. But then he tells me it's from a wound that got infected after he poked himself with a pencil during a math test in ninth grade.

"You mean on purpose?" I ask, and from behind me he confirms with a "Yup." When I ask why, he says, "I wanted to see how sharp it was," and I'm sure he didn't expect me to laugh as much as I do, but I don't think he minds it, either. Then he lays his scarred hand on top of my smooth one and says, "Your turn."

The laughter's loosened my insides. For a crazy, electrified moment I imagine telling him how I killed Patrick Mitchell and got away with it, only I didn't get away because you can't get away. How the urge to turn myself in gets stronger every day, only I can't turn myself in because it would mean turning my father in too, for *his* crimes—the legal ones, but also the sins of defying God and lying to the priest who was his best friend, and who knows, maybe others from that night I don't know about because he's sparing me.

If I told my father I wanted to confess, he'd be the first to support me. He'd drive me to the public safety building himself, let me describe to Steve Hinchey what happened that night, and then, so I wouldn't have to do it, he'd tell Steve how he destroyed evidence and obstructed justice to cover up my hit-and-run. Before long, Father Paul would find out how my father used him. Who knows what would happen between them then, but whatever it was, it would be a worse punishment than anything a judge could hand down. Which would be bad enough, given my father's condition.

So no, I won't go to the police. But things are closing in since this morning, and I can't just sit here and wait. I'd let myself forget Kelly's lighter for a few minutes while I was in bed with Griff, but it comes back to me with a rush, and I kick off the covers to jump up and yank on my underwear. "We really shouldn't be doing this, right? I mean, don't they say not to hook up with people from meetings?"

"Jesus, Jen. 'They' say a lot of things. It doesn't mean you can't decide for yourself." Griff rolls more slowly out of his side, and I can tell I've confused him again. "It's not like I'm proposing or anything." He puts his shirt on inside-out, curses, pulls it off and shrugs into it again. "Are you worried about your dad? What he'll think about you being with me?"

"I'm not 'with you.'" But I mumble it, because I'm not trying to be mean. "Why? Are *you* worried about him?"

"No." When he smooths his hair which doesn't need it, I sense he's soothing himself, and this makes me feel bad. "Not anymore. Hey, is he okay? I remember him as such a big guy, back when me and Cal hung together. I was kind of afraid of him. Now it's like he's—I don't know. What's the right word? Deflated."

It would hurt my father to hear him say this, but Griff's right. *Deflated* is the right word.

"The accident took a lot out of him." Only I know there was another accident, before the one that crippled my father on his way to church.

Griff pulls on his boots, stands, and stamps a few times to let the legs of his jeans settle. "Listen, Jen, you're not sorry, right? Please tell me you're not sorry."

At first I don't know what he's talking about, because I'm sorry for so much, but then I realize he means am I sorry about him and me. This. Being in bed together.

"No, I'm not sorry," I tell him, going over to lay a hand on his shoulder. When he reaches up to try to hold it there, I pull away. "But I can't do this, Griff. Trust me, *you* don't want to do this. I'm a train wreck. I'm damaged goods."

"So?" I can tell I've surprised him, by thinking what I said would be a surprise. "Who isn't?"

But I don't have to answer, because in the driveway we hear my father and Jerzy return. Griff sputters "Shit!" and offers to slip out the window, like we're characters in some romcom, but I tell him to be a big boy and come with me to meet the men in the kitchen. Jerzy blushes and looks away as he realizes what they walked in on, but if I'm not wrong I catch a small smile on my father's face.

"He just came by one last time," I tell them, and I see it takes Griff a second to get that I'm referring to a final check on the fire. Griff says we should be good—well, not *good*, but he feels confident issuing an all-clear—and he wishes us luck with the rebuild, then shakes my father's hand before clumping out to the night.

I ask my father about Sammie and he says there are some good signs, but it's still too soon to tell. He tells Jerzy he'll need another ride soon, because he wants to go relieve Bridget after a shower and a meal. Jerzy says sure, he'll just pop home and be back in a half hour. After he's left, my father nods at where Griff stood and says "I wouldn't have put you with him," and I say, "Why? I can see whoever I want," and he says, "Jennifer. I didn't mean you *can't* see him. I just wouldn't have guessed he would be your type."

He sits down heavily at the table, letting the cane drop, and I see what a toll the day's taken on him. Who am I kidding? It isn't only the day. "Griff and I aren't together," I say. When he raises his eyebrows I add, "I mean how would you think I could ever *be* with anyone?"

As soon as I see the effect these words have on my father, I want to snatch them back. It's a blow I've delivered to a man already down. For all the figuring he did about how to save me after I killed Patrick Mitchell, somehow this escaped him—the way our secret would ruin me for a relationship, not being able to confide in anyone what I've done.

He trapped me, when he drove into the tree at St. John's. But I'll never tell him I feel this way, because didn't I trap him before that, when I knocked on his bedroom door to tell him I'd hit someone with my car?

My father would say no. He'd say he doesn't get trapped into anything—whatever he does, he does because he decided to do it. Not because somebody else told him to, including God.

It's true, I never told him or asked him to fake an accident and lie to Father Paul. But it's also true that he'd still be going to St. John's, and still riding and running the stable, if I hadn't hit Patrick Mitchell after drinking beers on the beach.

I apologize to him for my tone, reminding myself what he's going through with Sammie, and switch on the Red Sox game. I offer to make dinner, but my father says he wants to do it, the old Luke Ripley made his own meals. With the hands he injured in his fall this morning, he pulls a package of ground beef from the fridge and starts cooking it up with some onions. When he stands at the stove his back is turned to me, which makes it easier for me to say, "I get it, keeping the lighter to ourselves. And not reporting Kelly. But how can we be sure she didn't do it because she knows what happened to Patrick? And won't go to the police?"

"If she had anything to take to the police, she would have done it already." He spoons the meat and onions onto two plates and sets them on the table. "Besides, we don't know for *sure* she set the fire. Somebody could have stolen the lighter from her."

What I wouldn't give to believe him. When I was a kid, I believed everything he said, even after my brothers told me not to. You have to learn that kind of thing for yourself.

We eat in silence for a few minutes, then pause to turn to the TV and watch the replay of a home run. My father says, "Well, that's a relief. He was out for a long time." I don't know which player he's referring to, and he probably expects me to ask.

Instead I rub my favorite nick in the table and say, "We never talk about that night."

"We can, if you want." One thing about my father: his body may have slowed down, but his mind never misses a beat. "It's just that right now, with Sammie—"

"I know. Do you think she'll be all right?"

"I hope so."

I move my fork without eating. "Daddy." I haven't called him *Daddy* since before my mother moved away with us, and it just comes out. "Would you go back and change things if you could?"

"Well, of course I'd change that boy being run over." How like my father to say it this way in front of me, both in the passive tense and without naming the person I killed. "But after that, no. I'd do everything the same."

If I know my father, this isn't an answer he's coming up with in the moment. If I know him, he's thought about it for hours—days, nights—before now.

"The fire, though. If Sammie dies on top of everything else..." But this is a sentence neither of us wants me to finish. "That night took so much away from you."

"It could have taken a lot more from *you*."

About this I won't correct him. "Don't you think you could tell Father Paul by now? I'm sure he'd forgive you."

"He'd forgive me because that's his job. He'd forgive me as a priest, not a friend."

"How would you know?"

"I'd know."

"But at least he'd understand what happened. Why you don't come around. As it is—well, I can tell it hurts him."

A risk. Won't my father ask how I could know anything about what Father Paul might be feeling? But he doesn't. He just tells me he's made peace with it—the friendship was something he had to give up for something else. That's what life is, he says. You have to keep deciding what matters most.

"What about God?" I ask.

"What about him?"

"Did you give that up, too?"

He looks as if he wouldn't have expected me to wonder this, but appreciates that I do. He shakes his head and says, "No. I still talk to him."

"Do you believe he forgives you?"

"I don't ask." He pulls himself to a stand. "But I know he loves me." Then even though one of his legs doesn't work, he's out the door to meet Jerzy before I can ask him to give Sammie a kiss for me.

FAITH IS NOT A FEELING, IT'S AN ACT. I find this line scrawled in my father's handwriting on a piece of paper he's using as a bookmark, when I go into his bedroom to open his nightstand drawer. I don't know whether somebody else said the line first or he came up with it himself. Reading it twice, I realize you could interpret "act" to mean doing something, or what people in meetings call "acting as if," which is basically pretending.

It sure sounds like a slogan from a meeting, but my father doesn't go to those. And it sounds like something someone might say in a time of despair, when he couldn't feel God around him. Is it a line he scribbled down in those days after I killed Patrick Mitchell and he made sure I didn't get caught? Or maybe it was after he had his own accident on the way to church, and understood he'd never walk right or ride again.

After he left to return to Sammie, I sat in the living room for a half hour or maybe more. The room faces the road, and when cars come around the curve they light up the trees just beyond the house. Even though I know better, I'm always afraid whoever's driving those cars can see inside, but tonight I didn't even think about it. Who cared? So what if they saw a young woman sitting by the window, fidgeting with her long hair as she stared out at the dark? From the expression on her face they'd know she was trying to figure something out. They'd know she was worried, but they'd never guess about what. They'd imagine a breakup, maybe, or anxiety about an exam. Maybe they'd send a quick hope or prayer her way. The idea made me want to cry. I don't believe in God anymore, or at least I don't think I do, but I believe people want the best for each other. And we want to be good, not only for God but for good's own sake.

Was *I* good? When the question passed through my mind I stood quickly, cleaned up the dishes, and opened my father's nightstand drawer. I wrote him a note, finishing with the request that he call my mother when he got it. For a few seconds, imagining that phone call, I considered throwing the note away and going to bed. Then I remembered how I feel waking up every morning, got in my car, and drove away from the house trying not to feel spooked by the empty space where the barn used to be.

It's pretty easy to figure where Kelly Mitchell will be on a Friday night in this town. She's at the soccer field behind the middle school with other kids, drinking beers behind the metal bleachers the parents petitioned for back before my family split up. My brothers all played on teams, and my mother signed me up for the Bean Sprout league without asking. She just assumed I wanted to do everything my brothers did. She was right, but I announced I was quitting the day I got smacked in the face with the ball. My father talked me out of it. "You can quit if you really want to," he told me. "But I hope you won't make it a habit to give things up because you're afraid."

Kelly appeared for her first day of horse therapy last month, when it got warm enough to start using the outdoor rings. She came in the van from the program for at-risk kids, and I knew her name because it was there on the clipboard with all the others. But—maybe because it served me not to—I didn't make the connection until she was standing right in front of me, and I recognized her face from that night. Or not from that night, but from the photo of Patrick Mitchell on the news the day after I killed him. They looked alike, except that in the photo Patrick was smiling, and in front of me as I led her to Sammie, Kelly was not.

What put her at risk? I wondered, after I got over the shock of realizing who she was. Had she been at risk before her brother died? And at risk of what? I knew Patrick's father took off after the funeral—I heard that around town. And her mother passed some bad checks, though most people gave her the chance to make good on them once they realized who she was and what she'd been through.

But none of that was my business when Kelly showed up that day. My job was to match her with a horse, show her how to groom it, and introduce her to whichever counselor had been assigned her case.

Patrick had been fair and so was Kelly, but his hair was straight and short, probably cut right before he had his picture taken at school. Kelly's had the look of hair that had been braided wet and slept on to create crimped sheets falling to her shoulders. I used to do that in high school myself sometimes—kind of a home perm. She hunched in an oversized denim jacket and wore wide-leg jeans, and I sensed she was one of those girls who hates warm weather because it makes it hard to wear the big clothes they prefer to hide their bodies in. That day and every time I saw her, Kelly wore blue Smurf studs in her ears. I wanted to tell her they were cute, but I worried it might embarrass her. Besides, I had no right.

I felt her staring at me as I checked her name off. Some of the girls did this, and the counselors said they might see me as a role model, since I was only a few years older. At first it unnerved me, but then I got used to it. "I remember when your brother died," I told Kelly, trying to sound casual.

I knew it was reckless but I didn't stop myself because I wanted—needed—to see how she'd react. "I'm really sorry."

"That's okay." She said it without any emotion, and I figured she thought I meant it the way everybody else did: as an expression of sympathy. Of course she couldn't know I was apologizing for killing her brother. "He was kind of a doofus, anyway." I sensed it was a line she'd delivered before, maybe her default response to receiving condolences. I turned away so she couldn't see my face.

Kelly was afraid of Sammie, to begin with. Most of our clients start off afraid, and they should; that's a twelve-hundred-pound creature we're asking them to make friends with. But fifteen minutes in, like everyone else, Kelly was patting the mare's mane and whispering things only Sammie would hear. That's the magic of horses. The miracle. They're as powerful as any other thing big enough to hurt you, but their power lies in their peace.

At the middle school, the grass glistens with night dew as I make my way across the soccer field. If I closed my eyes and listened, it might be the sounds of my Bean Sprout teammates I hear calling to each other behind the bleachers as I approach. What I wouldn't give to go back to them. But my eyes are open, and I know it's a bunch of teenagers I'm sneaking up on as they settle in for an evening of beer drinking and busting each other's chops.

I locate Kelly right away, sitting in a camp chair on the far side of the circle, wearing the same jeans jacket over a *Star Wars* tee. She gives a start when she sees me, her feet in their Converse knockoffs shuffling a quick dance below her seat. All the kids go quiet, the way they would for an adult. Then I remember that to them, I *am* an adult.

"Uh oh, Mitch," one of the boys says to her, "What'd you do now?"

Kelly tells him to fuck off, and I expect her to say the same to me after I ask if I can see her for a sec, keeping my voice light and nice—the voice she's used to hearing at the stable when I check her in for therapy. She points to herself and says, "Okay, see?" and tries to laugh, but it's way too lame and the rest of them have lost interest.

I walk around the outside of the circle and say to her, in a low voice, "Trust me, you want to keep this private." A boy in front of me snickers and hoots, "Lesbo alert!"

Something in my voice must make Kelly think it's in her interest to listen. When I motion for her to get up and come with me, she makes a show of being put out, sets the can of beer down, stands, and tells the girl sitting next to her to save her place. "I'll know if that's light when I get back," she says, nodding at the beer, but the girl just laughs, picks the can up, and chugs.

"Bitch." Kelly laughs too, but there's a nervousness in it. "If I'm not back in five, tell them I got kidnapped by a psycho horse chick."

More laughter follows us as we leave the circle and at first I think it's about me, but then I hear boys exchanging insults and I remember what it's like to be in high school and out drinking beer on a Friday night—the whole point is to bounce from one thing to another without any of it meaning anything.

Kelly trudges a few paces behind me to the other side of the bleachers, then across the field until we're standing under the floodlights in the parking lot next to my car. "We having a session?" she asks, her tone a mix of snark and worry. "How'd you fit Sammie in the trunk?"

I tell her Sammie got injured in the fire we had at the stable today. "You heard about that, right?"

Kelly shrugs. Or is that her shoulders trembling? "Yeah, I heard."

"You heard? Or you know because you set it?"

She didn't see this coming—she looks a hundred percent surprised by the question, which throws me a little. Could my father have been right, and someone else started the fire?

But she's not smart enough to realize that what she says next gives her away, by virtue of not being an answer. "Why would you accuse me of something like that? Why would I set a fire at the stable?"

"I don't know. That's why I'm asking." I move a little closer, and she takes the same number of steps back. "Maybe you waited till all the horses were outside. But you know you could have killed them, right? Some horses run back into burning barns." After a beat or two I tell her, "That's what Sammie did."

Kelly flinches. I watch her eyes move from one side of a decision to the other. Then she lands on one and says, "Well, a horse isn't a human. Which *you* killed one of."

The world goes white and my legs give, as if I've been kicked hard behind the knees.

"You probably didn't know I had two brothers." Her voice gains weight with each word as she sees me falter. "The other one, the one you *didn't* kill, works at Guidry's. When Pat died, Scott knew to be on the lookout for someone to bring in a wrecked car. Yours was the only one that showed up around the same time with the front end smashed."

Everything in me tries to keep my expression neutral, but I have no way of knowing if I've succeeded or not. "Right. My father had an accident with my car. He was driving to Mass and he had a medical event."

"Bullshit." But is that a flash of distress I see when she imagines my father hurting?

Then I remember the way she peered at me when I checked her name off last month, during her first visit to the stable. It wasn't because she was sizing me up as a role model. It was because she saw me as her brother's killer. "If Scott thought he had something to use against me," I ask, despite the pinpricks of alarm I felt warning me not to, "why didn't he go to the police?"

"He did."

What? I reach out to touch my car then stop, not wanting her to see I need the support.

"But he waited till the end of his shift," Kelly says, rolling her eyes like a little sister, "and somebody fixed the car before he could stop them. Steve Hinchey told us he knew your father ran into the tree by the church, and anyway, it was Luke Ripley we were talking about. He told Scott, 'Luke Ripley has regard in this town. He has standing.'" She hisses the word. "I mean, Pat didn't have any 'standing.' He was just a doofus who wanted to fix people's toilets someday." She laughs, but it sounds nothing like the laugh she gave her friends behind the bleachers.

What made me think this would go the way I imagined? If I should have learned anything by now, it's that things don't. Again, ignoring the internal signal to beware, I say, "If you suspected me back when it happened, why wait till now to set the fire?"

I can see she's torn. She doesn't want to incriminate herself, but she wants me to know the answer. In the end she splits the difference and says, "I told you I didn't set any fire. But why should *you* get off Scotch free? With horses and your father and that. It's not fair."

Scotch free! If only she knew. I remember the look Kelly gave my father the day she flicked the lighter at the barn and he asked her to put it away. Most people would have yelled, seeing a flame so close to the hay and their horses, and I remember feeling impressed—even if it didn't surprise me—that he managed to sound benevolent in delivering a command. I remember thinking she'd tested him. And he passed with higher marks than she'd even hoped.

Then I catch on to the gift she's offered without realizing. "You know *why* my father has that regard Steve talked about, right? Why he has 'standing'? Because people know he always does the right thing."

"Bullshit," Kelly says again. "The right thing changes depending on who you love." She hugs herself tight in her big denim sleeves. "I know you killed Pat, even if I can't prove it. I know what your father did for you. I didn't set your fire, but even if I did, you can't prove it either. So we're—well, not *even*. But whatever." She turns to start back to the safety of her circle across the field.

"Wait," I say, reaching into my pocket. When I pull out the half-melted Zippo, I see under the floodlights every bit of color drain from her face.

"That's not mine," she says, but it's too late, she's given herself away and besides, the damn thing's stamped with her initials. "I mean yeah it's mine, but somebody stole it off me." Does she think I don't notice her surreptitiously patting her jacket's chest pocket, desperately hoping to find the lighter where she thought it would be?

"Kelly. Listen to me." I cast around for my horse-therapy demeanor—sympathetic and in charge. "I came to find you because we can help each other."

She gives a *pfft* that tries to sound dismissive. But now she knows she hasn't gotten away with something she thought she did, and I've got her attention. "Help each other how?"

"I need you to do something. In exchange, I won't take this to the police." I hold up the Zippo and I can tell she considers trying to swipe it from me and run, but the moment passes and she's still standing there, thinking. "Just get in the car," I tell her, opening the passenger door. "Come for a ride."

"Yeah, right. Like I'd get in a car with *you*."

Of course. Why hadn't I thought of that? If I had thought of it, I might still be home looking out the window. I apologize and tell her it won't take long—five minutes, tops. When she doesn't make a move, I wave the Zippo in front of her. "Either come with me, or I get in alone and drive this straight over to Steve."

She stands there hugging herself even tighter in the April chill. Calculating. I can feel her from the inside—gut churning, thoughts escaping before she even knows they're there.

Then she throws up her hands to surrender and pitches herself in the passenger seat. "Thank you," I say. Can she hear the relief in my voice? I tell her not to worry, she'll be home soon.

"Home," she repeats, as if the word means nothing to her. As if I'm teaching her a foreign language and this is one of the hardest sounds to pronounce.

"What's with the Smurfs?" I ask, idiotically trying to put her at ease, and she looks at me like I'm insane. I gesture at the studs in her ears and she puts her fingers to her lobes as if to remind herself what's there.

"It's a joke. Pat never gave me anything for my birthday growing up, but once he got a job, my mother told him he had to. So he got me these to bust my chops, because he knew I'd never wear them. And I didn't, until he died." She caresses the surface of the one in her left ear. "What the fuck do *you* care?"

There's no answer to this she'll believe, so instead I tell her to put on her seatbelt. She gives a scornful snort. I peel out of the parking lot and we drive by a cornfield that hasn't been planted yet, then the Dunks where everybody gets their ice coffee before school. A mile or so more and we're coming up on St. John's, where I see a light in the rectory and imagine Father Paul in there watching something on Netflix, one of those spy movies he likes.

It occurs to me that it's not too late to stop this. I could turn around and drive Kelly back to her friends. We share a secret now—*two* secrets—and neither of us is going to tell either of them. I could go home and rip up the note I wrote my father, wait for him to come and give me the update on Sammie. He wouldn't ask me about Kelly's lighter or what I did with it. We'd talk about the new barn we'll build, how maybe this is a blessing in disguise because we can make those improvements we've been putting off. He'd tell me we can start over.

But then we'd say goodnight and go to bed and then it would be morning. And I know I told Griff I'd be there, but the truth is I don't have another morning in me of going to that meeting and acting like somebody who's doing everything she can to get better.

So instead of turning around as we pass St. John's, I tell Kelly the story of how my brother hid in the tree and dropped raisins on people's heads at the strawberry festival. When I get to the part about Cal trying to escape punishment by saying "It was *raisins*," she makes a sound that might be another version of a laugh, but it's hard to tell.

In the center of town, where the river runs behind the public safety building, I drive back and slow down just enough to open the window and hurl the lighter over the rail, toward the water we can hear but not see. I say to Kelly, "Deal?"

"What'd you do *that* for? How stupid are you?" Her dark eyes flash with excitement. "Without that, you got nothing on me."

"It doesn't matter." I accelerate back toward the road. "When they stop us, you can tell them whatever you want. I hunted you down to accuse you of setting the fire. Or you have no idea why you were kidnapped by a psycho horse chick. It's up to you." I take the turn too fast, and she snatches the grab bar above her seat. "All they need to know is you didn't want to get in the car with me, but I had a gun."

"A gun." She snorts again. "Yeah, right."

My backpack's on the console between us, the front pouch unzipped. I reach over and pull it open, telling Kelly to look. When she sees my father's pistol she sucks in a breath so big it comes out again in a howl.

Does she have any idea how hard it was for me to take the Glock out of the nightstand and put it in my pack? How much I hate holding it? My father showed me how to use the gun when he got it, in case I was ever home alone when somebody broke in, but that was months ago and I haven't touched it since.

"I'm not going to hurt you," I tell Kelly, closing the pouch again. "It's just a prop."

"What the fuck does *that* mean?" Kelly twists to see if there's anyone outside whose attention she can attract. The sidewalks are empty, but it doesn't take long once I speed up twenty miles over the limit for a police car to appear in my rearview, flashing its lights. Kelly flings herself back against the seat and shouts, "What is this? Are you trying to kill us both?"

No. The opposite.

Would she listen if I advised her to confess to setting the fire? Save herself suffering? Of course not. She'll find out the hard way, same as me.

Besides, I'm in no position to save anyone but myself. When the siren screams behind us I push the gas, sending the needle so fast and so high Kelly shrieks at me to stop, slow down, what am I doing? "You're crazy, you know that? You're out of your motherfucking mind."

She might be right. Is it crazy to trust something you can't be sure is there?

Faith is not a feeling—it's a blind dive off the edge.

When the police car's close enough I slow down, pull over, and park before the bridge. In the mirror I watch Steve Hinchey approaching, his walk and manner wary until he sees it's me behind the wheel. He smiles, and I wait for him to make a joke about my joyride. Then beside me Kelly blurts, "Get me *out* of here, she has a *gun*" and everything changes, starting with the face of the man who doesn't want to but will arrest me now because he has no choice.

Cri de Coeur

Before the man with the bottle appeared, there were things I wanted to say but no one was listening. How did this feel? I leave it to you to guess.

When I was young, there was nothing I dreamed of more than "becoming" a writer, by which I meant I wanted to be famous for novels and stories that touched people and also impressed them, by virtue of my elegant prose and insights about the human condition.

I'd published my first book and was in my thirties before I even began to question whether my worth as a person, not to mention my happiness, depended on what I might publish and how well it might be received. In other words, I knew better by then, but I still allowed myself to believe that a big book would deliver the life I'd dreamed of.

And might qualify me for an obituary in *The New York Times*, the headline of which I woke up imagining on the morning of my fifty-fifth birthday: *Regina Morse, Whose Fiction Career Soared in Midlife, Dies at 75.*

I had twenty years left to write the big book! I could do that, right? And didn't the fact that it came to me in a dream mean it might be my destiny?

The only problem was that I wrote small books, not big ones. Either I would have to figure out how to write what would be considered a big book, or what was considered a big book would have to change.

The things that happened to people in my stories were not things you could observe—the shifts occurred inside them, because the characters grew tired of being themselves. They knew change was required, but not how to go about it. Usually, I provided them with a choice they recognized as one that could, if they played their cards right, lead to their salvation.

Well, "salvation" might be too strong a word—it wasn't always do-or-die, at least not literally. But it's fair to say most of my characters suffered a cry of the heart at the forks in their roads.

When that first collection of stories came out with a (small) literary publishing house, I thought, *Look out, world, here I come!* Only one more book and twenty-five years later, I found myself approaching my desk not with excitement and hope, as in the old days, but trepidation. I was irrelevant or redundant—take your pick—or both. Nobody was reading my work. I knew this because of the sales figures and because when I searched library databases, my two little volumes were always available, everywhere. The few reviews I received in obscure places used words like *veiled* and *muted*, when I had hoped for *compelling* and *taut*.

I was okay as long as I allowed myself to believe that people were reaching for stories with more explosive external plots. The audience for quiet, internal transformations would always be more select, I told myself. But those readers would appreciate my work all the more! Where I ran into trouble was when a quiet book did well in the world—took off, even—at which point I had to consider that maybe I just wasn't as good a writer as I thought I was. *Who do you think you are, Gina—Chekhov?* The question kept me away from the typewriter for days, because most certainly, I was not.

And maybe ordinary is the same thing as boring, Gina—did you ever think of that? Well, in fact, I had. I mean it wasn't boring to me, but maybe I wasn't the best judge.

The dismay and despair I felt about my own fiction began to extend to what I felt about everyone else's. Whereas words on a page—my own or another's—once had the capacity to contain color and movement and life, now I saw only static black marks on white backgrounds, strung together in an order I knew was supposed to make me feel something, but instead left me dead inside.

That may not sound like much. I'm not describing a critical injury or illness. Except that for a reader and writer, it sort of was. I tried to transfer the ambition I'd previously felt about my creative work to my job writing standardized exam questions, but you can probably imagine how long that lasted.

It wouldn't have mattered so much if I'd wised up sooner and invested in love. But I thought it wouldn't be possible to have or do both. Why was this? I both knew and knew of good and respected writers who had partners, which was one thing, and even children—quite another. Not just men, but other women. I'd always believed I wouldn't be able to write, if I were a mother. That everything my reservoir was filled with, I would owe to the kids.

Had I been wrong? Could it even have been the case that the commitment to nurture other people would have helped me nurture my work? Would the reservoir have grown deeper and wider if I'd been part of a family, a household routine featuring shared meals and bank accounts, drop-offs and pickups, dance recitals and soccer games and a measure of fatigue that would have forced me to learn how to rejuvenate myself?

The thought filled me with even more despair, which I hadn't thought possible. Because at this point, there was no going back. There were no do-overs. I'd bet on the wrong horse—myself—and now I was stuck with it, for better or (as I already knew the case to be) worse.

A MAN WITH A GOATEE CAME TO MY DOOR peddling an elixir he promised would make me feel better. Take away whatever worried or angered me, infuse my system with a lightness and energy I wouldn't find anywhere else. (*Which system?* I should have asked. *Nervous? Digestive? Immune?*) I knew better, but on the other hand, I figured I didn't have anything to lose. It was just for kicks—right? If nothing else, it might give me something to write about. I had some disposable income, and not much I felt excited to spend it on. I paid him the money and he gave me the bottle, which was unlabeled, made of brown glass, and the right size to contain about twelve liquid ounces. I shouldn't overdo, he told me; I should just sprinkle a few drops on my eggs each morning.

"I don't really eat many eggs," I told him. The truth was that I didn't eat much of anything, anymore.

Well, he told me, a few drops in my coffee would also do the trick. If I wanted to give him my contact information, he'd follow up in a month or so to ask about my results.

Ha! I thought but didn't say. *You'll be in touch to try to sell me another bottle.* I declined his invitation to provide my email address or phone number.

The whole exchange had a movie or dream quality to it, down to what the guy looked like, dressed all in black except for a red tie, with makeup accentuating his eyes and a hat of the kind men don't wear anymore. But I could feel the weight of the bottle in my hand. After I'd shut the door behind him, I poured myself another cup of coffee, opened the bottle, and sniffed the dropper. No smell. What if it was poison? It wouldn't be poison—right? There are cameras everywhere nowadays; the traveling elixir salesman would have been traced in a heartbeat if I was found dead and they did an autopsy and found some weird toxin in my blood.

I squeezed in a few drops and stirred. "Bottoms up," I whispered, then took a sip. It will tell you something about my state of mind and heart—see above—that the idea of poisoning myself was not, as the saying goes, a deal-breaker.

There was no discernible taste. Was it water? It could have been water, right? I finished the coffee and sat down at my desk, waiting for the elixir to kick in. The salesman hadn't said anything about when this might happen, so why shouldn't I hope for some immediate effect?

In my typewriter was a sheet of paper containing my latest efforts at a new story. I read the words there and instead of the usual plunging sensation, I felt a lift at once familiar and foreign, which is to say that my body recalled the pleasure of creating without having actually experienced it in a long time.

Woot! What *was* that stuff? I didn't feel disoriented or numbed at all, the way I would have with an intoxicant. I sat at my desk for the next three hours and finished the story, then retyped it into the computer so that I could submit it to one of the journals that routinely rejected my work these days. Ordinarily I would have set it aside to revise later, but when I read it out loud to myself, I knew it was solid and ready to go. I uploaded it to five sites I considered stretches, rolled a fresh sheet into my typewriter, and started another story. The next time I looked up, the sun was setting, and my inbox contained an acceptance of the manuscript I'd submitted only hours earlier.

Was I dreaming? I knew I must be. Either that, or my debilitated psyche had propelled me into a state that only seemed like reality. When I woke up, or came to, or recovered enough to understand this, I'd go back to my dread of approaching my desk and rolling a fresh sheet of paper into the typewriter, only to sit and stare at it with paralysis and shame.

But though I waited for this to happen, it did not. I made myself dinner, and afterward read three chapters of a novel I'd been saving for when I could appreciate it. My taste for both food and reading had returned; though I knew I'd been depriving myself because I had so little appetite for them, I hadn't realized how desperately I'd missed both.

WITHIN SIX MONTHS I'D PUBLISHED NEW STORIES in both *The New Yorker* and *Granta*, gained eighteen pounds I couldn't afford to have lost in the first place, and been offered the position of Visiting Distinguished Writer at the state university system whose flagship campus was in my own city. It was a prestigious program, and they assigned me the most advanced workshop of juniors and seniors. They'd all read my work, and came to every class session eager to ask questions and discuss both my stories and their own, which were earnest and ambitious if a bit derivative, but that seemed par for the course—desirable, even—with undergrads. Babies learn to speak by imitating the adults around them, right?

I loved sharing with my students the things I believed about fiction. Some of these I enjoyed writing on the whiteboard, such as "Ambiguous ≠ Profound." I quoted Toni Morrison to them: "If there's a book that you want to read but it hasn't been written yet, then *you* must write it." They took notes and hung on my every word.

You may be wondering what changed, in my stories, for them to suddenly be snatched up like that, leading to all this success. Well, nothing. That's what was so amazing. For whatever reason I couldn't guess, there seemed to have been a literary sea change—had it happened overnight?—in the tastes of fiction readers and, as they say, influencers. Epic royal fantasies took a back seat to stories about regular families. Faeries and demons gave way to dentists and clerks. Instead of escaping, people wanted to plunge into depictions of experiences like their own. Garden-variety humanness appeared to be back in vogue.

The students lapped up the readings I assigned them, like the Chekhov story about the carriage driver whose son has just died and whose only wish is to find a sympathetic listener; when people keep blowing him off because they're impatient or cold or just don't want to hear a sad story, he ends up expressing his sorrow to his horse. The story's title is "Misery" and sometimes it's also called "To Whom Shall

I Tell My Grief?" and it gets me every time. This time it got my students, too.

The story I'd finished writing the night I took the first elixir dose was about an unconfident college boy who manages to get a popular girlfriend by virtue of his academic success. On their first weekend trip together, he asks if she'd mind their stopping off to visit his grandmother, because his mother has asked him to. The girlfriend is less than thrilled by the prospect, but agrees. During the visit, the grandmother breaks wind standing up from the table, and the girlfriend laughs. Later, the boy can't bring himself to go through with the sex the girl initiates on their romantic getaway, because he's so bothered by the laugh. The girl turns irate, mocks him, and storms off. Alone, the boy feels like a fool, at the same time understanding he couldn't have done anything else.

A "small" moment, yes. The obscure reviewers were right to use that word about my work. But suddenly people seemed to want to read about such moments, more than they wanted to read about murder investigations and magic schools. I gave my students a writing prompt for an in-class exercise: *A grandmother embarrasses herself by farting. Go.* Oh, the scenes they wrote and shared that day! Some comic, as you might imagine. Others focused on the piteousness of the scenario, as my own story had. We laughed a lot. There were a few tears, too. On their way out, they thanked me for reminding them of how much power can lie in the plainest things.

The improvements in my life didn't end with my professional success and physical recovery. I even met a man I liked, who seemed to like me back (to use a phrase I remembered from my middle-school days). Instead of cutting bait after two or three dates because I was so afraid it couldn't last, I allowed myself to know him well enough that when he asked if I wanted to move in with him, it wasn't a surprise to hear myself saying *Yes*.

How lucky am I? It was a mantra that came to me daily. How many people get second chances at… everything, as I did?

I know you're wondering—because anyone would be—how much of the bottle was left. I know you're thinking that I'd been mixing in a drop or two with my breakfast every morning all this time, and you've concluded that of course it wasn't the elixir itself but a placebo effect that accounted for all the good things that had happened in my life since the morning I met the elixir salesman. Well, about the first you'd be right: I did continue using the drops, but they ran out after the *New Yorker* story and before the one in *Granta*. It would be dishonest of me to say that I didn't panic, a little, when I squeezed the dropper one morning and it made a squirting noise but nothing came out. I thought about hanging onto the bottle, but since there wasn't a label and it was now empty, I didn't see the point other than for sentiment's sake, and I've always prided myself on not being sentimental ("Sentiment ≠ Poignancy").

I myself didn't consider the bottle's contents and the magic that followed as a placebo effect, but I *did* see them as connected. The funny-looking salesman had arrived one morning when I was at my lowest point, and after he left, the very idea that I had paid good money for something to make me feel better—when I'd known all along that this task was in my own hands and nobody else's, and certainly not in a drop of what was probably water—jump-started me, in the way I'd needed jump-starting for a long time. It caused me to recognize the inertia I'd given in to, and raise arms against it. Begin taking charge of my own fate. So I guess you could say that the man who appeared at my door *had*, at least indirectly, cured me…

My new beau, Paul, had a daughter in her thirties and though I wasn't technically her stepmother she latched on to me quickly, having lost her own mother a few years earlier. Danielle lived in the city and worked at a job she hated, selling social media ads. She shared an apartment with roommates she hated, who partied every night and kept her from getting enough sleep. Her father worried about her. "She doesn't have what it takes to get herself out of it," he told me. I said I knew something about that condition (giving the impression it was ancient personal history) and I'd do anything I could to help, and he thanked me.

He asked when my movers were scheduled, but I told him I hadn't hired any, because his place had everything I needed except for clothes and a few favorite books. I packed those up and sold my furniture to the couple who'd be taking over my lease the next day, then sat at the kitchen table to drink my last cup of coffee in the rooms where I'd been so unhappy for so much of my life.

BUT BEFORE I'D DRAINED THE MUG I heard a knock and there he was, the elixir salesman. His previous visit was so distant from my thoughts that I didn't recognize him at first, though clearly he recognized *me*. Which was a surprise because I knew I looked different, having gained weight and gotten happy. He was dressed the same—black shoes and black clothing, set off by the thin red tie—but he'd shaved the goatee, and the eyes he'd previously rimmed with kohl now appeared naked, almost as if he'd been crying.

After a few seconds I understood that I'd met him before, but before I could place him, he cried out, "Marvelous! The elixir appears to have agreed with you!" and of course *then* I knew, because elixirs are not something one comes across every day.

I asked him if I could buy two bottles, because it had occurred to me that I could give one to Danielle. It was just what she needed! I would sustain the good life I'd found for myself, and she'd begin the journey down her own prettier path.

But the salesman said he only had one bottle left. I asked if there was surplus in another location—a warehouse, perhaps, or a distribution center—but he shook his head, expressed his regret, and told me the price had tripled from last time, because they were running out. "We only had so much to begin with," he said, when I asked if they'd be manufacturing more. "Nobody remembers the recipe. It was an accident the first time, so unless the same accident happens again, we're all screwed."

Ignoring the queasiness I felt when he said this, I paid the sum and took the bottle, and he went on his way. I still had half a cup of coffee left from my breakfast, and I thought about adding a drop or two to it, but realized I'd have to save it, stretch the liquid, to make it last.

I'd bought the bottle thinking I would give it to Danielle, because I didn't believe in elixirs and knew I didn't need it myself, but I also knew what my investment in the fantasy that it *might* work had done for me before I met her father, and I thought the same might be true for her. Paul and I were supposed to meet her in the city for dinner that night, so I put the bottle in my bag and thought about how I would present it—as a lark, I figured: a piece of whimsy we'd laugh about. A year from now, though, she'd take me aside and thank me, still laughing, and say she knew she shouldn't believe in fairy tales, but ever since I'd made a gift of the elixir, her life had been looking up.

First I planned to present it during our appetizers. Then I figured I'd wait for dessert. But somehow, the meal came and went without my reaching into my bag to draw the bottle out. Danielle was in a state, even sobbing briefly at the table as she confessed to Paul and me that she couldn't stand her job or her apartment anymore; she asked if she could move in with us until she found new versions of both. Paul was alarmed, I could tell. I felt it, too. Yet still I did not reach for the bottle, even as I told myself I should.

And not only did I not give it to Danielle that night, I squeezed out a few drops for myself the next morning. Was it true that I didn't believe that whatever was in the bottle was responsible for the good fortune I'd enjoyed during the last two years? Yes. But was it also true that my fortune had changed only when—if not because—I bought the bottle and began consuming its contents? Also yes.

There were still things I wanted that seemed potentially out of reach (A Pulitzer! A wedding!), not to mention that the salesman's most recent visit triggered a fear at the back of my mind that maybe the elixir was capable of wearing off. I couldn't risk returning to the state I'd been in before he showed up the first time. After I moved into Paul's place I didn't look back, and things were mostly fine until the night Danielle had a blowup with her roommates, told them she was leaving, and informed us that she was moving back into her old room for a while.

It wasn't a big apartment. Her "old room," which became her new room, lay on the other side of the wall from ours. And when a week after she moved in she quit her job and said she needed "a break" before finding a new one, she was home just about all the time.

It wasn't long before this caused friction between her father and me, severely cutting into the time we spent together doing the things we enjoyed, like working crosswords and watching movies. He almost always invited Danielle to join in, and she almost always accepted. I avoided going home at my usual time, staying later on campus than I needed to or browsing in bookstores long after I found what I'd gone there for. On weekends, to get her out of the house, Paul often made reservations for the three of us upstate somewhere. I loved exploring and I loved Danielle—I did—but I missed the intimacy Paul and I had enjoyed before she moved in. I didn't bring it up, though, because I knew he worried about her mental health, and I figured the arrangement had to end sometime.

Wasn't that what being a good partner meant? You compromised and put up with things that were important to the other person, even if they were a drag for you?

I'm sorry to say I became less and less agreeable about it all. Eventually, Danielle got a therapist and a part-time job, and I was excited about the prospect of being alone in the house with Paul sometimes, but as it turned out, both of these things she did remotely. When the fall semester started, I signed up for tutoring shifts at the language center, which kept me out of the house until after dinner two nights a week and on Saturday mornings. Paul and I started fighting—in earnest now, not just the spats we used to be able to weather because we both apologized before they could get out of hand; these were full-blown, drawn-out, take-no-prisoner sieges. I lost sleep, and this affected my performance in the classroom.

Worst of all, when I sat down to write, nothing came. My hands hovered over the keys. Sometimes I'd type "The quick brown fox jumped over the lazy dog" over and over, thinking the activity of my fingers would stimulate activity in my mind, but I usually just ended up with a page of that one stupid line, which I crumpled up and threw away and then got yelled at by Danielle for not recycling.

A student reported me for a microaggression after a class session in which I offered the opinion that writers shouldn't be restricted to writing about characters only like themselves—that fiction is by definition an imaginative art, to which there are no boundaries. All pain is the same, I said. In this I was quoting Toni Morrison again, but that didn't seem to matter. Word got around. The dean suggested I take a "sabbatical" the following semester and concentrate on my own work, but it would not be a paid sabbatical, and I knew it meant my contract would not be renewed.

It took me longer than it should have to realize that I was being punished, and to understand what I needed to do—what I should have done a lot sooner. The next morning, I took the bottle of elixir from my pocket and squeezed multiple drops (more than my standard dosage) into Danielle's orange juice. But before I could bring it to her at the table, Paul said, "What the hell was that?" and took the glass away from me.

Danielle got up, yawned, and retreated to her bedroom for therapy. Paul waited until she was out of earshot before he started in again. "You put something in her drink, without asking?"

"It's not what it looks like," I said.

"Well, it better not be. Explain, Gina, please."

But how could I explain? I did try. I started with a recounting of how miserable I had been—unable to write or in any other way flourish—before the man appeared at my door and sold me a bottle identical to the one I carried now in my pocket. I pulled it out to show Paul and he examined it closely, removing the dropper and sniffing it, searching for an ingredients label that didn't exist.

"What I don't understand," he said, "is how you could believe in a magic potion."

"It's not a 'magic potion'! It's an elixir." But even before the words were out, I knew this was no leg to stand on. "I *don't* really believe in it, I swear. But things changed so much—everything got so much better—I figured it didn't matter if it was just a placebo or not. Either way, it *worked*."

I expected him to smile and sympathize. I expected some gentle mockery. What I wasn't prepared for was the expression of incredulous scorn I saw on his face. "You know this is crazy, right?" he asked. "Absolute, downright…"

"Okay!" I grabbed the bottle away from him. "You don't have to be mean about it. Look, it's no different from the Tarot cards your sister read at Thanksgiving."

"That's just for entertainment. She doesn't believe in them. No one does."

"Fine. It's probably just water in here, I know. Are you satisfied?"

"Not until you pour it down the sink."

"But what if it could work for Danielle the same way it worked for me? Not for real—not chemically—but because she *thinks* it might make things better?"

A cloud crossed Paul's features. "If you actually thought that might happen, why didn't you offer it sooner? You know how bad things are for her. You kept it for yourself, when my daughter's suffering?"

"I knew she'd think it was crazy," I told him, though that wasn't the reason. "I knew *you* would. You just used the word 'crazy' a minute ago."

"That's not what I'm talking about." He shook his head. "I'm talking about a lack of generosity on your part. A kind of... selfishness I haven't seen before."

"You're not being fair!" I shouted, loud enough to bring Danielle running from her room.

In the end—because it *was* the end—I did pour what remained in the bottle down the drain, but the gesture came too late. I was left without both the life I'd been able to make for myself, and the formula that brought it about.

I didn't worry too much at first, because I figured the salesman would appear again. He had to appear again, right? In a fairy tale, everything comes in threes.

But no knock came my way. No salvation.

BY NOW I'M SURE YOU'VE GUESSED that there was never a traveling salesman at my door, or any elixir. I mean, come on: an *elixir*? No publishing in the places I'd always dreamed about, and no elevation in the numbers of people clamoring to read the small, quiet stories I wanted to write. No students I looked forward to mothering—I mean mentoring—every day.

What you might *not* have guessed is that there was no Paul or Danielle, either. No move to a bigger apartment with a better view and another heartbeat to keep my own company. The good news is that I didn't have to go through a breakup, I didn't get reported for a classroom indiscretion, didn't surrender my apartment and end up with no place to go. I didn't lose any love.

Now I understand that there's not going to be a big book, or, when the day comes, an obituary in *The New York Times*. This morning I got out all the beginnings I've written over the years, of what I hoped might turn out to be a bestseller. I see that I'd tried to fashion stories around hostage situations, murderous children, identical twins buried in beach sand—even a drug cartel! What was I thinking?

Eventually I incinerated them all, came back to my desk and rolled an empty sheet into the typewriter. Could you write a story like Chekhov's now and get away with it? Well, of course you could *write* it—in fact, it's the very story I'm writing here. But would it get published?

You search and search for a person who'll listen, and in the end you cry your heart out to your horse.

But it's not as bad as all that for me. It's not as if I don't have people, because I do—like the grandmother who rising from the table farts then blushes, and the grandson who gives up the girl cruel enough to laugh. The grandson could have been my own someday, though I don't, as the saying goes, go there. Whatever realm they belong to and however small it might be, my characters move me. Their stories do. And just because they're fiction doesn't mean they aren't true.

Acknowledgments

Many thanks to editors Steven Schwartz, Stephanie G'Schwind, Megan Sexton, Carolyn Kuebler, Elizabeth McKenzie, Marc Berley, Tony Huang, Soma Mei Sheng Frazier, Edward Delaney, Gordon Krupsky, Grant Tracey, and Jeremy Schraffenberger for publishing the following stories in the journals in which they first appeared: "Cliché" in *Colorado Review*; "An Early Departure" in *Five Points*; "Tribute" in *New England Review*; "Attached" in *Chicago Quarterly Review*; "An Interest in History" in *LitMag*; "Infusion" in *Hong Kong Review*; "The Boy on the Skateboard" and "Take What You Want" in *Subnivean*; "First Day" in *Mount Hope Magazine*; "Undefeated" in *The MacGuffin*; "The Forest" in *Solstice Literary Magazine*; and "Ride Share" in *North American Review*.

Special appreciation to Nicole Lamy and Celeste Ng for selecting "An Early Departure" for *The Best American Short Stories 2025*.

For their specific contributions to individual stories, I'm deeply grateful to Ann Treadway, Philip Holland, Adam Schwartz, Karin Lin-Greenberg, Sadie Johnson, Daniel Johnson, Molly Johnson, Katie Gergel, Laura Gergel, Jack Gergel, Michael Dondiego, Mary Karr, Elizabeth Searle, Marianne Leone, John Skoyles, Eileen Pollack, Elizabeth Berg, Marja Mills, Julie Bolton, and Julia Keller.

My thanks as well to my family, friends, colleagues, and students at Emerson College for their continuing support and good cheer. Thanks in memoriam to Nancy Zafris, who loved short stories, wrote beautiful ones herself, and championed mine at a critical time in my career.

Thanks to Jean Williams at Cary Memorial Library, Sophie Jones at Art Resource, and Daniel Trujillo at Artists Rights Society for their help in securing use of the book's cover image. Thanks to Kimberly Witherspoon and Jessica Mileo for their sustained and faithful representation of my work.

To Dr. Ross Tangedal and everyone at Cornerstone Press, my gratitude for giving this collection such a thoughtfully curated home.

Elizabeth McCracken is responsible for the delicious description of the difference between a novel and a short story quoted in "The Boy on the Skateboard." Robert Fanning graciously granted me permission to quote Bill Knott's transcendent poem "Death" in "Tribute."

Finally, admirers of Andre Dubus's work will recognize characters he created, for his story "A Father's Story," in "The Daughter's Story," which is intended to be both companion and homage.

JESSICA TREADWAY is the award-winning author of seven books, including the story collections *Absent Without Leave*, *Infinite Dimensions*, and *Please Come Back to Me*, which received the Flannery O'Connor Award for Short Fiction. Her fiction has been published in *The Atlantic*, *Ploughshares*, *The Hudson Review*, *Glimmer Train*, *AGNI*, *Five Points*, and other journals, and has appeared in *The Best American Short Stories*. A Senior Distinguished Writer in Residence at Emerson College, she lives in Lexington, Massachusetts.

www.ingramcontent.com/pod-product-compliance
Lightning Source LLC
LaVergne TN
LVHW040053080526
838202LV00045B/3615